COLTON

KENTUCKY GREEN - BOOK 1

OLIVIA SANDS

D1714176

OLIVIA SANDS

INTRODUCTION

She's all wrong for him.

So why can't he stop thinking about her?

Colton Green knows *exactly* what he's going to do with his life. He'll run the Red Widow Bourbon factory—a business that's been in his family for generations—build a beautiful home, marry a nice country girl, and start a family.

Then he meets Grace Baker, and all his plans go out the window. She's the last woman he should want: a big-city lawyer who's accepted a case against his best friend. There's no reason to think she plans to stay in Elm Ridge, let alone that she wants to settle down with the likes of him. Still, he's drawn to her like he's never been to anyone.

Grace Baker is trying to put her life back together after the disastrous end of her marriage. She needs to heal, not fall headlong into a new relationship. Colton may be easy on the eyes, but the last thing she's looking for is romance.

Besides, Grace knows she's a bad bet all around. A close-knit family like the Greens is something she's never experienced, and she doesn't belong in their world ... no matter how much it makes her heart yearn.

Can Colton put aside his preconceptions for the woman who just might be perfect for him? And can Grace let herself believe she's worthy of real love?

Welcome to the small town of Elm Ridge, Kentucky, where you'll swoon, smile, and fall helplessly in love with the Green family. This heartwarming romance has no cliffhangers and no cheating.

FOREWORD

Each book in the KENTUCKY GREEN small town romance series can be read on its own.

You can become a member of Olivia's **VIP readers group** to get goodies and news at https://oliviasands.com/BM

You can also follow Olivia on

* her site

https://oliviasands.com

* Facebook

https://www.facebook.com/OliviaSandsAuthor

* Instagram

https://www.instagram.com/oliviasandsauthor/

* Twitter

https://twitter.com/byOliviaSands

CONTENTS

CHAPTER 1

GRACE

Barely ten past two, and already both sides of the fork in the road leading to Ashton Green's farm were filled with parked cars—pickups, expensive cars, and massive SUVs. By New York standards, the monsters would be considered trucks, not passenger vehicles.

Observing the long line, Grace made a mental note: in Elm Ridge Kentucky two-ish means two on the dot.

Parking in an open field between two local monsters, Grace noticed that the wheels of those things were higher than the roof of her treasured Mini Austin Cooper.

Another note to self—she'd been doing that a lot lately—determine if she needed to swap her cute little car for a more serious vehicle or if her baby would be fine as long as she didn't get lost on a dirt road or sandwiched between two monsters.

Wine bottle and bag in hand, Grace smoothed her blouse and patted her rebellious hair tucked neatly in a business-like bun. A backyard Memorial Day barbecue held at her new boss' McMansion, the invitation felt overwhelmingly official.

Though he did say it would be casual. Her outfit was casual. She thought it was. She was breaking in new boots with a spring skirt. She'd also packed a cardigan in her bag, just in case it got cooler later. Smoothing her blouse unnecessarily one more time, she stopped herself.

Come on woman, you can do this!

A crackerjack at her job, there was no reason to be nervous. She could ace social too. She could. And if she repeated that enough, she just might learn to handle her personal life with the same efficiency as she managed her work.

Instinctively, her gaze dropped to her left hand. Traces of a failed marriage vanish faster on ring fingers than they do on the soul.

Voices and music led her along the road uphill until a turn revealed a large clearing. Dead center stood a ginormous house.

In front of the house had been set up for a picture-perfect gathering. Lined up into two rows, she counted a dozen picnic tables covered with white and red checkered tablecloths.

From the road, she searched through the crowd gathered around an open bar and, not recognizing anyone, sucked in a big breath.

She froze and considered retracing her steps back to her car when someone called her name.

"Grace!"

Looking around for the source of the voice, she finally spotted a familiar face. Ashton Green, her boss, waved at her from the largest barbecue pit she'd ever seen. Grilling for a small army on that thing would be a piece of cake. She'd been in New York apartments smaller than this set up.

Armed with very long forks, two very tall guys younger than Ashton stood beside him flipping huge pieces of meat without breaking a sweat. Clad in denim jeans and slightly buttoned-down shirts, rolled-up sleeves exposed capable arms. She couldn't help staring at the men. Not just men. Every girl's fantasy cowboy in the flesh.

Handsome, tall, rugged, swoon-worthy.

"I'm so happy you could make it," Ashton Green said.

"I wouldn't have missed it for the world." Happy that her voice didn't betray her raw nerves, she might have exaggerated a bit.

Her first impulse had been to spend the three days of the extended weekend curled up on the beat-up sofa of her furnished rental with a nice novel, or maybe if she had felt adventurous, she might have surfed online for blackout curtains for her too-bright bedroom.

If she was going to build a new life in Elm Ridge, she needed to become a social animal again. Basically, she needed to get a life, and that wouldn't happen if she remained hidden under the covers. The invitation won over the impulse.

"Boys," Ashton said to his two assistants, "meet Grace Baker. She joined my firm a few weeks ago, and I still can't get over how lucky I am to have snatched her away from the big city."

"Thank you, but I'm the lucky one." This time she meant it.

Desperate to get away from Manhattan, she'd had no idea where to go. And then, by accident, she'd stumbled onto his ad. At the time, she'd thought it divine intervention.

Incredibly, there was a human-sized law firm in a small town looking for a non-belligerent general practitioner. Yep, the ad was every answer to her prayers.

"Grace, these handsome devils are two of my nephews," Ashton said. "This is Jaxon. He's a horseman."

She shook the hand Jaxon extended. Rough and calloused,

just how she'd imagined a cowboy's hand would feel. His sky-blue eyes shone with kindness.

"Nice to meet you, Grace." He flashed a magnificent smile filled with warmth.

"Very nice to meet you too," she answered. "A horseman?"

"What he means is that I breed horses and run an equestrian training facility."

"And this year he's opening it to kids," Ashton added.

Before she had a chance to ask anything more, Ashton continued with the introductions, "And this fellow here is Colton, a Bourbon man."

Colton's skin was as smooth as his brother's was rough and his eyes darker than night, the deepest shade of chestnut she'd ever seen. Frowning, he shook her hand and studied her face intently.

Before she could ask what being a Bourbon man entailed, Colton asked, "So you think you can adapt to country life?"

"I'm sure going to give it my best shot."

"Interesting." Still holding her hand, he tilted his head as though memorizing her features.

Strangely, the prolonged contact didn't feel awkward at all, possibly because she was drawn in by his thoughtful gaze.

Calling them back to reality, Ashton broke the spell. "Colton, your steaks!"

Slowly letting go of Grace's hand, Colton flashed her an apologetic grin and turned his attention back to the grill.

"Let me introduce you to the rest of the family." Ashton caught her arm and escorted her away from the fire.

Glancing over her shoulder, Grace noticed Colton had dutifully returned to his task of cooking meat while Jaxon, with an amused smile, watched her and his uncle walk away.

What had just happened? Had she ever felt such an instant connection with anyone? Maybe not, but one thing was for sure, Jaxon had noticed too, and from the look of him, it was making his day.

Oh well, whatever she imagined she saw—real or not—Grace was only interested in making friends. Just friends.

She'd learned the hard way, she couldn't be anything more. After all, she was damaged goods.

CHAPTER 2

COLTON

"Don't say it," Colton barked at his brother.

He didn't even have to look up from the meat on the grill to know Jaxon wore an insolent smirk—one Colton would love to wipe from his face.

"I wasn't going to say a thing."

Colton glanced at his brother for a second, noticing the expected smirk and his eyes riveted on Grace's back and her gentle sway. Couldn't blame him really, it was a lovely sight.

Setting the cooked burgers on a plate, he handed it off to Jaxon. "Take them to the buffet table."

So lost in his own thoughts, Jaxon didn't respond. Colton wasn't the only one who couldn't keep his eyes off Uncle Ashton's latest recruit. Too bad she wasn't his type.

Not that he or his brothers had a type per se. Heck, they'd been pretty eclectic in their choice of dates, especially in college. But they did favor gentle souls, and one thing was for sure, Ashton's lawyers were no such thing. Just the opposite, in fact. He prided himself on hiring *cutthroat lawyers*.

"Earth to Jaxon," Colton called out.

"Nah, I'm good here." Jaxon's head jerked in his direction,

"You take the tray, and while you're at it, why don't you see if the pretty new lawyer wants a burger."

"Not my type, bro." He jiggled the tray in front of his brother.

Shaking his head, Jaxon retook his station behind the grill, grabbed a spatula, and faced his brother. "Then no reason you can't take her the burgers."

"Fine." Tray in hand, he turned on his heels and walked away. The problem wasn't type, it was temptation.

Uncle Ashton's new protégée appeared a bit overwhelmed. Still clutching the bottle of wine with a red bow tied around its neck like a lifeline, he suspected she had meant to offer it to his uncle. Maybe the legal eagle had a little nervous filly in her.

By the time he reached her side, Uncle Ashton had already made introductions to Colton's parents and his Uncle Mason. Talking a mile a minute, it was obvious to anyone in the family that Uncle Mason had instantly adopted her.

"You're awfully pretty for a lawyer," Mason blurted with his usual childlike sincerity.

For a split second, from the shock in her eyes he expected some sort of retort. Instead, a sweet smile took over her face.

"That is maybe the nicest thing anyone has said to me in a very long time."

Uncle Mason beamed. Uncle Ashton nodded approvingly. Score one for the city lawyer, especially since most people had little patience for Uncle Mason.

"Would anyone like a burger?" Colton held out the tray.

"Oh, thank you." Smiling more sincerely than before, she accepted a burger and a paper plate and turned to Uncle Mason. "Would you like something?"

Sporting the brightest smile he'd seen in a long time, his uncle nodded. "Yes, thank you, I would."

Score two for the city lawyer.

"Colton get your backside over here. Now," his sister Sophia called out from inside.

"Excuse me." Colton handed off the tray and trotted towards the house, coming to a screeching halt at the sight of his sister wrestling with a keg of beer.

Huffing, Sophia looked up. "Uh, this is a little heavy here."

"Sorry. Why are you doing this alone?" He hurried to grab one end before she broke something. Like a foot.

"That's sort of what I was thinking." She nudged the keg toward her brother. "Apparently, most of this family is talking with, watching, or otherwise fascinated with Uncle Ashton's newest recruit."

He couldn't blame them. In only a few moments conversation, he'd uncovered a softer side to latest legal eagle—a side he was sorely tempted to explore before she hightailed it back to the city.

"Earth to Colton. You're not holding up your end."

Blast, he was no better than Jaxon, fixating on the wrong woman. Pretty smile and nice hips or not. "That's because you're supposed to lay it on its side to move it."

"Why didn't you say that in the first place?"

Because he was thinking about the legal eagle and her smile. "All right, now you know. Let's get moving."

Tilting the keg to its side, he contemplated her staying long enough for him to dig a little deeper. But what business did he have messing with that type?

Drafted by his Aunt Addison to help in the kitchen, not until desserts were served was he able to return to mingling with the guests.

Across the patio, empty plate in hand, Grace stared at the assortment of desserts.

"Cinnamon buns, snickerdoodles, or brownies?" he whispered from behind her.

Startled either by his question or his voice, she gave a little hop and turned to face him. A lovely shade of pink rose to her cheeks. Colton was pleasantly surprised. She was like a kid caught with her hand in the cookie jar.

"Well, that's a tough one," she answered.

"The buns are homemade. My aunt's specialty." He held one up for her to get a good look.

"It does look delicious." She stared at the scrumptious pastry. "But the thing is ..." Frowning, she hesitated, "Can I tell you a secret?"

He nodded. If she was ready to share a secret with a perfect stranger, it couldn't be much of a secret, and even if it were, keeping secrets was only one of the things he was good at.

"I have to confess..." She hesitated again. "And I know it's almost sacrilegious, but the thing is…" She glanced over each shoulder and back to him. "I really, really hate cinnamon."

"How can you not like cinnamon?" His voice rose an octave. He glanced down at the table and back at her. "It's almost un-American."

"I know," she whispered sheepishly. "I'm deeply ashamed of myself, but it's terribly frustrating that so many of the most popular desserts are laced with cinnamon."

Shaking his head, he held back a chuckle. "When you put it that way, I guess you'll have to go with the brownie. Sophia baked them this morning. Sadly, the snickerdoodles are store bought."

"Sophia... That's your sister, right?"

"You must have been introduced to a good fifty people today." Colton handed her a brownie. "I'm impressed you remember."

"And I forgot most of their names a few seconds after I

heard them," she confessed. "Though your Uncle Ashton did make it easy to remember his daughters' names."

"How so?"

"Well, he did name them in alphabetical order." Grace closed her eyes and recited, "Audrey, Bailey, Cora, Darlene, Elisabeth, and... Faith."

He laughed and applauded. "Most people don't notice."

"Now, your parents on the other hand have made it very confusing." She frowned as she asked, "Is there a tradition in your family that all men's name must end in *on*?"

"You noticed that too." He was starting to like this woman. Not good.

"It would be hard not to!" she protested. "When Ashton introduced you and your brother Jaxon, I thought it was an amusing coincidence, but then I met a Landon, a Mason, a Braxton, and a Hudson, and I realized it couldn't be an accident."

Her amused expression teased a broader smile out of him. He considered telling her that his brother Weston's best friend was named Nelson and thought better of it. No need to add to the tsunami of new names she had to memorize today.

"You think it's funny, but it's really confusing, because right now I can't remember who's who. I should have taken up Gloria's offer to give me a cheat sheet!"

He laughed again. Gloria was Ashton's office manager, the first secretary his uncle had hired when he hung his shingle, and if someone could draw an accurate family tree, she'd be the one. She knew everything there was to know about the Green tribe. Not that they were hiding any nefarious secrets but, like with every family, there were things they'd rather keep to themselves.

Colton helped himself to a brownie as well, escorted Grace

to an empty table, and pulled out a chair for her. "Would you care for a refresher course?"

Shielding her face from the sun with her hand, she looked up at him and bestowed him with a smile as warm as the one she'd shared with Mason.

"I would like that very much. And then you could tell me what Ashton meant when he said you were a Bourbon man."

"Oh, you're going to wish you'd never asked." He rolled eyes skyward. "If there's one subject I can talk about for hours, it's Bourbon!"

Actually, right about then, he'd gladly talk about any subject and use any excuse to be around her.

CHAPTER 3

GRACE

Immersed in her most interesting new case, Grace almost jumped when someone knocked on the frame of her open door.

"Come in," she said while attempting to finish the paragraph she was reading.

"Grace!"

Oops, she was being rude. *Manners, young lady!* She looked up.

Gloria stood in front of her desk, hands on her hips, a perfect figure of matronly reprobation.

"Yes, Gloria," she answered a bit wearily, wondering what she could have possibly done to upset her.

"Do you know what time it is?"

"I'm not sure." A quick glance to the planner open on the corner of her desk reassured her she hadn't missed an appointment or meeting. She had purposely kept her entire afternoon open to really dig into this new file. "Why do you ask?"

"Because it's now six thirty."

"And?"

"You should be gone by now! You're not in New York

anymore. You're not required to bill a gazillion hours a week." Gloria sighed and took one of the two seats across from her. "Honey, you need to get out of here."

Grace shook her head and smiled. It hadn't taken her long to figure out that the hours kept at Green and Partners were not the ones she was used to in Manhattan. These people did work hard, but it wasn't all they did. They made time for themselves and their families.

Grace had also figured out that even though Gloria ran a very tight ship, she was all about flexible hours and adaptable schedules. As long as the job was done and one could be reached in case of emergency, she didn't care if you took three hours for lunch. Grace had seen two paralegals do it— one to get a new hairdo and the other to go hold her widowed cousin's hand as she started her chemotherapy. Stuff like that never would have happened in Grace's old firm.

"I won't let you burn yourself out on my watch." Her scolding tone was adorable.

"I promise I won't, but..." How could Grace admit that she didn't have anything better to do and that she'd rather be here, studying this estate dispute, than home staring at her walls? The furnished rental they had found for the duration of her trial period was adequate, but it was not a home.

"Yeah, yeah, I get it," Gloria said. "You're new in town and you haven't made friends yet, so you figure you may as well stay here, but you don't get it, do you?"

Grace shook her head. *Apparently not.*

"You won't make friends if you spend all your evenings alone in the office."

Her knee-jerk reaction was to accuse the pot of calling the kettle black. After all, still here at this hour, Gloria didn't practice what she preached. So instead of barking back at her as she would have a few weeks ago to anyone who would have interrupted her work, Grace agreed with her.

"You're absolutely right," she conceded.

"You'll realize soon enough that I usually am," Gloria answered good-naturedly.

"I am sure I will." She slid a folded sheet as a bookmark into her file before closing it shut.

Visibly satisfied with her answer, Gloria stood and was about to leave when Grace held her back.

"Gloria," she asked. "Do you have any special plans for tonight?"

"I was planning to visit the Gumbo La Ya to check out the band."

"Is that the créole place?" Grace had heard others in the office talking about it.

"The best in Elm Ridge! And they have the best music too."

"Live music?"

"Right as rain. Every Friday night they do."

"Would it be okay if I tagged along?"

Gloria's smile lit up her face. "I thought you'd never ask."

Ten minutes later, they were in a rather large and busy restaurant. For an instant, Grace thought they would never get a table, but then in the back of the room someone stood and waved at them.

"Oh, here they are," Gloria said, pulling Grace through the crowd. "This is where all the cool kids hang out on Friday nights."

Grace liked that answer. It made her a cool kid too!

She counted seven women already nursing colorful drinks. Two of them were Gloria's age, probably in their fifties. The others looked under thirty. She was introduced to everyone. Re-introduced to some of them, actually. There was a summer associate and a paralegal she had already met at work and two members of the Green family, Audrey, her boss' oldest daughter, and Sophia, her cousin.

Sophia introduced her to another young woman, Willow, her 'bestie' she said, giggling like a teenager. "She's in Elm Ridge for the summer."

"And those two older kids," Gloria looked at her contemporaries, "are the coolest ones of the lot."

"We are indeed," said the first one, a larger than life Dolly Partonish woman. "And don't let anyone tell you otherwise, 'cause the two of us, we rule this town."

The woman she pointed to was her exact opposite, a creature so petite Grace was ready to bet she had to look for her clothing in the children's section of department stores.

"We do," the miniature woman concurred.

Gloria laughed. "They can indeed make or break anyone in this town."

"Hello, Grace, I'm Sandy Ball," said the blond bombshell. "I get to decide who looks good and who doesn't."

"She owns the Ball salon across from your offices," Sophia explained.

Grace shook the hand Sandy extended, even though it did look like a deadly weapon. She'd never seen such long nails. The blood-red lacquer shone brightly under the spotlight like sharpened blades. Grace thought her a little scary.

"And this is Doctor Nayar." Sandy let go of her hand. "She decides who lives or dies."

"Stop being so dramatic," the doctor said to her friend. "And please, call me Chandi."

Her handshake was surprisingly strong for someone so little.

"Nice to meet you, Chandi," Grace answered.

"Chandi runs Elm Ridge's medical center," Gloria

explained, and then looking at Sophia she added, "a medical center which will soon offer the services of a freshly graduated nurse practitioner."

Sophia nodded with enthusiasm. "I actually started today."

"Congratulations!" Grace took the empty seat next to Willow, Sophia's friend.

"So many new beginnings," Gloria noted, taking another empty chair.

"Ah, to be young again," Chandi said wistfully.

"You're kidding, right?" Sandy protested. "Don't you remember how awkward and clumsy we were?" She shrugged in mock horror as she picked up a menu from the pile the waitress had dropped on the table. "Boy, I'm glad those days are behind us, though one thing's for sure, I'm going to enjoy watching this new generation come up with new ways to mess up their lives."

As they picked up their menus, Willow and Grace exchanged a look and silently agreed — Sandy was scary.

The cardboard menu boasted the sort of food Grace imagined they served in New Orleans—chicken étouffée and jambalaya and gumbo—but she'd never had créole food before. She had no clue what to pick.

"Do you need help choosing?" Audrey asked.

"Oh, absolutely."

"Well, it all depends on how spicy you like your food."

"I think I'm in the mood to test something hot." Grace couldn't believe she'd just said that!

She had no idea what had come over her, but she didn't take it back and let Willow talk her into ordering the hottest jambalaya. Up until now, her food had been like her life, bland.

It was high time for her to spice things up.

CHAPTER 4

COLTON

"What do you think?" Standing in front of the building, Veronica twirled for Colton.

"Nice," Colton said easily. His assistant always managed to look spectacular. "Real nice."

Uh-oh! From the scowl on her face, he could tell his answer wasn't satisfactory. *Come on, Colton, you'll have to do better.* He raised his hands in a defensive gesture. "Let me rephrase that. Marilyn Monroe has nothing on you." He held his breath, fingers crossed, hoping he'd said the right thing.

She smiled and twirled again, her blond curls bouncing on her shoulders as her red dress rose showing her perfect legs. "That's better. With another ten years of training, I may teach you how to pay a proper compliment to a girl."

"If you fail, it won't be for lack of trying." He opened the door of his pickup for her.

"So, do you think my date will like it?" she asked as soon as he had buckled up.

"Of course he will. He would have to be crazy not to." The jerk du jour was many things, but crazy wasn't one of them. Why couldn't she see that the new man she was madly in love

19

with was egotistical, self-centered, and couldn't possibly love anyone but himself? Veronica deserved better. He wished she'd keep looking. There were plenty of fishes in the local pond that would want nothing better than for her to catch them in her net.

"You don't like him, do you?"

That was the understatement of the year, but Colton knew better than to tell her what he thought. "Let's just say that he's not really my type."

She laughed and let it go. "No, your type would be curvier with darker hair, right?"

An image of Grace popped into his mind, and he couldn't help but smile.

They had barely made it onto the main road when she turned to him. "You know, Colton Green, I really feel sorry for you."

Wow! Colton had no idea where this was coming from. He glanced in her direction.

"There's no passion in your life!"

"I beg to differ. Remember how excited I was when we landed us that new distribution contract? And what about the time we finalized our new packaging?" From the corner of his eye, Colton watched her shrug away his comments.

"Don't play dumb boss, you know what I mean."

He did. "If what you mean is that I'm not as passionate as you are, then I have to admit you're absolutely right."

If anything, Veronica was too passionate. Usually, Veronica's passions were as intense as they were brief. She met the guy, thought the world of him, imagined herself walking down the aisle with him, and then *poof*, her eyes opened, and she realized he was not the perfect man she'd envisioned or imagined. When she did, she didn't mourn. She turned around and said, "Next!" Fortunately, she was just as passionate about her work. He would have to be the crazy one to complain about the way she threw herself into everything she did at the office. She was his right hand, and he had no idea what he'd do without her, especially now that Weston was away.

"You bet I'm passionate. Meeting Elton is the best thing that has happened to me in a long time. Wait a minute, don't tell me you're jealous?"

Uh, oh. Surely, she didn't think his dislike for Mr. Rockstar Wanabee had anything to do with his being afraid of losing her? "Don't be ridiculous. You may be the best darned assistant I ever had, but if this guy was good enough for you and wanted to sweep you away on his white horse, I'd be the first one to cheer you on."

"Wow, maybe you are more passionate than I thought. The thing with you is that you keep everything all bottled up inside. But mark my words, one day you're going to meet that one girl that will turn your life upside down like Elton does for me. For all I know, she won't even tick off half the requirements of your checklist."

She was so adamant that Colton chuckled.

That's when she frowned and shook a finger at him. "Oh, my Lord, I knew it. You do have a checklist!"

Pulling into the parking lot of the restaurant, he unbuckled his seatbelt, happy to escape any further analysis. It saved him from explaining that even if he did have a checklist, which he didn't, there was really nothing wrong with his knowing what he wanted. In the few seconds it took for him to walk around the car, she'd returned her focus to the singing idiot again.

He helped her get down from her seat and took her arm to walk into the overcrowded restaurant. From the looks of it, Elton did indeed draw a crowd. What did he know? Veronica could be right about the man's talent. They made their way past the long bar into the sitting area, and he scanned the room looking for his sister's table. Spotting it, he pulled Veronica behind him and led the way.

"Here's Elm Ridge's most eligible bachelor," Sandy, the self-appointed queen of Elm Ridge teased.

His cousin Audrey winked in his direction. "Flattery won't get you anywhere with him."

Bringing the back of her hand to her forehead in dramatic despair, Sandy sighed. "Oh, the things I could do with such a beautiful head of hair."

"I know, I know," Chandi told her gently. "But you know how his mother is. Julia won't let anyone else cut any of her sons' hair."

"What about Weston?" Sandy protested.

"Even Weston," Sophia answered. "Mom shaves his head every time he comes home on leave."

"And if Uncle Sam can't beat her, you don't stand a chance," Gloria concurred.

Colton waved at her. "If anyone would be privy to the family idiosyncrasies it would be Gloria. Considering how long she's worked for my uncle, she knows all our quirks."

Leaving the ladies to console Sandy for never getting the male members of the Green family to sit in her hairdressing chair, Colton turned to say hello to the rest of the table. He nodded and smiled to two women he didn't know and walked around the table to go hug Willow. She and Sophia had been besties since they started college, and he really liked the young woman.

It took Colton a few seconds to recognize the woman sitting next to Willow.

"Hello, Colton. It's nice to see you again."

"Grace?" he gasped like a landed fish as she pushed an

incredible mane of dark curly hair to one side of her neck and looked up at him.

Veronica stepped between him and Grace, offering her hand to Willow and then to his uncle's new associate, saving him from embarrassing himself by saying something inappropriately stupid.

Willow shifted over a seat, leaving an empty space between her and Grace.

"Care to have a seat?" Grace pointed to the empty chair.

Veronica shook her head and cooed, "Nah, I won't be staying. You see, I'm the lead singer's girlfriend, so I get to watch the show from backstage."

Calling the tiny room adjacent to the Gumbo La Ya scene a *backstage* required a stretch of the imagination but, hey, if it made her happy, no one would contradict her.

Veronica turned around, and before she sashayed away, she whispered in Colton's ear, "Ooh, I like the way you look at her. Maybe there's hope for you yet!"

CHAPTER 5

GRACE

Colton took the seat between Willow and Grace.

"So, the two ladies from New York ended up sitting together," he said. "Are you nostalgic for your hometown?"

"Oh, absolutely not," Willow protested. "Ever since Sophia invited me to visit the first time, I've loved Elm Ridge and dreamed about finding a way to move here for good."

"Why don't you?" Colton asked.

"I'm considering it," Willow answered.

"Good! We need more warm and cheery people like you around." He turned to look at Grace. "And what about you?"

"It's only been a few weeks, but I'm as happy as can be."

Gloria leaned over in their direction. "Why wouldn't she be? She's now living in a delightful little town instead of a horribly crowded city and working for the best firm in all of Kentucky."

"Where do you live?" Colton asked.

"In a furnished rental for the duration of my trial period," Grace told him.

"You can find furnished rentals in Elm Ridge?" Audrey seemed genuinely surprised.

"Of course you can!" Gloria answered. "I find some each year for our interns and summer associates. There's always a few families happy to take in some boarders and people who move out of town for a bit who are delighted to rent out their places to Green and Partners."

Audrey nodded. "Of course. I guess I never thought about it before."

The speakers overhead crackled announcing the start of the show. The lights dimmed in the room, and all eyes turned toward the stage. The first musician to appear, a young man, adjusted a swiveling chair between some sort of electric piano and another keyboard instrument. He tested his setting to make sure he could comfortably reach both and then looked up to the other man, slightly older, who plugged in his guitar and came to stand in front of a mike.

"Is that Veronica's new beau?" Sophia whispered.

"If it is, the girl has impeccable taste," Sandy cooed.

Colton rolled his eyes and sighed.

"The man is drop dead handsome," Audrey chimed in. "And let me tell you, he can sing too!"

The man opened his mouth and in three notes proved Audrey right. His voice was like velvet, and Grace could see why any woman could instantly fall in love with him.

The two-man band started with a lively song, and within minutes the dance floor filled up. Sophia, Audrey, and Willow were among the first to jump on it. They invited Grace to come along, but she declined.

Colton faced her. "You don't dance?"

It had been years since she had a chance to test her dance floor legs, and she had no intention of making a fool of herself in front of him. "Not on that sort of beat."

Her answer was rewarded with a smile that lit up his face. "I hear you. I favor country music myself."

Grace looked back to the stage. Colton was much more handsome than the singer. Veronica's boyfriend was too lithe for Grace's taste. Not that she ever needed protection, but she'd always been attracted to men with more physical substance—men like Colton. She glanced in his direction. The man did ooze testosterone.

A few songs later, the lights dimmed a little more, and the tempo of the music slowed down. Half of the patrons made their way back to the tables. Those left behind snuggled on the dance floor swaying with the slower rhythm. Colton stood and offered Grace his hand. She hesitated for a quarter of a second, but a little demon on her shoulder whispered in her ear, *"Come on Grace, get up and make new friends."* Right. That wouldn't happen if she stayed a wallflower.

She stood and followed him. They passed a breathless, but smiling Willow. Coming from the opposite direction, she winked at them. Colton was spot on when he called her warm and cheery. That was precisely the vibe she gave off. Willow was one of those people for whom there were no strangers, only friends she had yet to meet. Grace was a bit jealous, but she shouldn't have been. It was up to her to change and become less guarded. But she was making progress, wasn't she?

The second her feet hit the wooden floor, Colton eased her into his arms. He held her close, but not too close. His hands were warm. They rested comfortably on the small of her back, and she could feel his heat through the thin fabric of her dress. For an instant, she looked up and they stared into each other's eyes. Was it dark enough to hide the fact that his thoughtful gaze made her blush? Unsure, she hid her face by resting her cheek against his chest. He pulled her in a little closer, and she breathed him in. He did smell heavenly, fresh and manly. He felt good.

Too soon the song ended, but Colton didn't release her. A

new one began, and they continued to sway gently. It was really nice. More than nice actually. She cursed her brain that could never stop thinking. Why couldn't she enjoy the moment without over analyzing everything? The moment was lovely, and she should leave it at that.

Colton lowered his head and whispered in her ear. "What was the heavy sigh for?"

Without lifting her cheek from his chest, she whispered back, "Contentment."

"That's good. Excellent actually."

Yes, it was. But then it wasn't. Well, not really. Colton was way too charming. So charming that she could easily fall for him.

The second song ended, and they walked back to the table.

"Thank you for the dance," he said pulling out her chair for her.

"You're very welcome."

The moment became awkward when she realized all eyes were on them, and Grace felt herself blush again. Heat rushed to her cheeks, and wished she'd stop doing that. But then Sandy stood, took two steps toward Colton, and asked, "And what about going for a spin with an old lady?"

Thank you, Sandy.

For a second, Grace read disappointment in his eyes, but it vanished so fast that she thought she'd imagine it.

Smiling, he answered, "Well, I was going to invite you, but if you say I have to take one for the team, I will. Where is that old lady you want me to dance with?"

Sandy ate it up.

"Colton Green, you're a true gentleman," Sandy purred, patting him softly on the chest before leading him away.

Yeah, a gentleman and a charmer. A very deadly combination.

As soon as they walked away, Grace decided it was time to call it a night. She said goodbye to everyone with a special thank you to Gloria for such a lovely evening.

The same country tune they had just danced to a few minutes earlier filled the car when she turned on the engine. Placing her hand on the steering wheel, she paused to look at the building. It was a nice song, a nice dance, and a nice man.

Maybe deciding to be happy really was all it took.

CHAPTER 6

COLTON

Summer lunches were a big family tradition for the Green clan.

Uncle Ashton and Aunt Addison launched the season with his Memorial Day weekend barbecue, and Colton's parents got the big finale for Labor Day. They took turns for the Fourth of July. This year, it was Uncle Ashton's turn again. The idea made Colton smile. The man loved his fireworks.

When Colton was a kid, the family used to alternate between their two houses and their grandparents' home. Now that their grandparents were gone, the parents had been dropping hints about how, as they were growing older, all the kids would be expected—as they moved into their own places—to take a turn.

He had thought that wouldn't be for years since his parents weren't really that old. But then Jaxon had to go and volunteer to host a barbecue at his ranch last summer. He said it was no big deal for him since his home was huge. Running a training facility, Jaxon had the equipment to feed more than fifty people.

Colton still couldn't adjust to the idea that his brother

planned to turn it into a horseback riding camp later in the season. Jaxon had never had any patience with kids, and it was going to be interesting to observe.

Looking around the lawn at all the tables, Colton wondered how he would manage if he volunteered for a weekend.

"You look very thoughtful," Sophia said, plopping herself next to him on the rocking bench by the kitchen door. "Trouble in Bourbon paradise?"

"Nah, I was just thinking about taking on one of the Sunday lunches."

"Oh, in your house?"

He nodded.

Sophia tilted her head and frowned. "Well, that would be a challenge for you, wouldn't it?"

"Yeah, but I still want to do my part, you know."

"Have you considered teaming up with Jaxon?"

"How so?"

"You know, make it your weekend, but organize it at his place."

Colton gave her a big hug. "My sister, the genius!"

"Any time, bro." She shrugged as if it was no big deal when she'd actually found a way to make his life a lot easier.

Colton had no doubt that Jaxon wouldn't mind as long as they agreed on a convenient weekend, one that would agree with his plans.

"How's life treating you?" he asked his sister. "We never had a chance to talk on Friday."

"No, we didn't. You were way too fascinated by Grace," she teased.

Now it was his turn to shrug. Grace was a lovely lady, and he couldn't deny that he found her attractive, but... So many buts, he wouldn't even know where to start.

"And it's clear she really likes you too," Sophia encouraged.

"I don't know about that."

"Why do you say that?"

"Because she left without saying goodbye. Literally." He laughed. "So, you see, I'm not sure I made such a good impression on her since she felt the need to run away as soon as I turned my back to go dancing with Sandy."

Sophia's laughter was so spontaneous, Colton realized his answer may have been a bit too aggressive.

"Oh, you really do not understand women, do you?"

He chuckled. "I'm pretty sure I don't."

"That's okay, one day you'll figure it out." She patted his leg as she stood. "I don't have time to explain it to you right now 'because I have to take my pie out of the oven, but I promise you her rushing out like that is a good sign."

Really? Sophia was right. When it came to their interactions with men, he didn't understand how women thought. Colton had closely observed his female cousins, and their behaviors seldom made sense to him. He got that there was some set of rules to follow and that a nice girl couldn't very well go up to a guy and tell him that she found him interesting. In their neck of the woods, that would be very much frowned upon, but still, if a woman liked a man, why would she run away without saying goodbye? The truth of the matter was, he had been miffed when he had returned to find her gone.

The kitchen door slammed shut behind Sophia and then squeaked open again.

"There you are. I was looking all over for you!" Gunner came out onto the back porch.

"Hey," Colton answered as his best buddy took the seat Sophia had been occupying a minute earlier. "I'm glad you could make it."

"I almost didn't come."

Colton looked at him and gestured to encourage him to tell him more. Gunner loved all Green parties and always said he wouldn't miss them for the world.

"No worries. My issue is with your uncle, but as long as I stay clear of him, I'll be all right." Gunner smiled, but it didn't reach his eyes. He'd been stressed since his mom had passed.

Colton wished he could find a way to help him. "What's with you and Ashton?"

Gunner stared out into the distance. "Mackenzie has hired him."

"She's suing you?"

How do families ever come to that? Gunner's twin had always been a wildcard but still, Colton wouldn't have thought her capable of suing her own brother!

Then, what Gunner had said hit him. Mackenzie had hired Ashton?

How could Ashton decide to take a side and represent one of the two siblings when he'd known both of them all their lives? If he had to take a side, he should have stood by Gunner. After all, Mackenzie was the one who had left town, broken all ties, and crushed her parents' hearts.

"I'm not sure what she's doing," Gunner said. "The only thing I know is that I received a letter from Ashton's firm inviting me to some sort of meeting next week."

Colton jumped up from the bench, ready to charge away in search of his uncle to give him a piece of his mind.

Gunner reached out and grabbed his arm. "Please don't."

"But..."

"Nah," Gunner shook his head. "It could be much worse. Ashton's an honest man, and if I'm going to fight against someone, I would rather deal with his firm than with some out-of-state big shot who wouldn't understand the first thing about the way we run businesses here. But that doesn't mean I wanna talk to him now."

Colton cooled down and saw his point. Ashton was indeed a man of honor. He had no doubt that his uncle could be ruthless when necessary, but he also knew that Ashton would not do anything underhanded to harm Gunner.

"And don't you worry, I know my limits. If he makes me an offer, I'll run it through another attorney before I sign anything."

Colton wouldn't like to be in Gunner's shoes right now. He'd sacrificed everything to make the Cox Stud Farm what it was today. He'd worked day and night to grow it into a very successful business. For sure, his sister couldn't come waltzing in and reap half of the benefits of his hard labor for herself, could she?

"The only thing that worries me," Gunner leaned back, "is that the person I'm meeting with is a woman I've never heard about before."

"Oh, yeah?"

"Can't remember her name right now, but she must be new because I couldn't find anything about her on the Green and Partners web site. The only attorney I found by that name is in New York and practices ADR, whatever that is..."

Colton didn't know what ADR stood for either, but he had a bad feeling in his gut about who it was Gunner was supposed to meet. He was about to ask him if the attorney's name was Grace Baker when the porch door slammed shut behind Jaxon.

Shaking his head, Jaxon took a seat on the bench beside his brother, muttering "Remind me why I thought opening a summer camp was a good idea?"

Colton looked to his left and then to his right. The three of them sure looked like a sorry bunch.

Jaxon was lost in serious thoughts, no doubt wondering how he was going to deal with a camp full of kids in a few weeks. Gunner was stressed by the idea of a confrontation with his long-lost sister, and Colton... well, he was pretty sure the woman who was going to mess up his best buddy's life was the only woman who'd captured his interest in forever.

CHAPTER 7

GRACE

The Green and Partners firm boasted two conference rooms. One was cold and professional with a very long table and huge screens, the perfect place for holding corporate meetings or organizing closings. The second was more like a tiny living room with a small table and a pair of comfy L-shaped sofas.

When Ashton Green had given Grace a tour of the offices, he'd explained that years ago he had found that some negotiation worked better in a more intimate setting. She agreed that he was right, it made for a less hostile discussion when parents sat down to talk about child custody issues in a room that looked like it belonged in someone's home.

The Cox estate case seemed like the perfect opportunity for Grace to test the magic of that cozy place. Mackenzie Cox's reaction to it was positive. The second Grace showed her in, she ceased to clutch nervously at her large paper file and settled onto one of the sofas.

"This is nice..." she said, smoothing some imaginary wrinkles from her skirt. "Not what I imagined at all."

"We use this room for very special clients." Grace took a seat across from her. "Those we want to make comfortable."

"So, I am your client?" she asked. "Ashton was not very clear. He said he was willing to help me, but I couldn't hire him as my attorney."

Uh, oh... Interesting. Ashton had left it up to her to tell Mackenzie what he wanted to do in this case. "Have you heard about ADR?"

Mackenzie shook her lovely head and frowned. "Nope, I can't say that I have."

"Well, it stands for Alternative Dispute Resolution. It covers various methods that can be used to bring people together and help them find a common ground to settle their disputes," Grace paused to let the words sink in.

Unsettled, Mackenzie clutched her file again, this time so hard her knuckles turned white.

"Mediation is one of those methods, and this is the service Ashton is offering to provide."

"I don't understand," Mackenzie whispered, sitting up straighter on the edge of the seat.

"Let me explain myself better. Green and Partners will not be your attorney or your brother's attorney. If you both agree, it will act as your mediator."

"How does it work?" Frowning, Mackenzie leaned back into the sofa.

"If you both agree to a mediation, I will talk with each of you separately. I will explain to each of you what your legal situation is and then you will each tell me what is it that you want." Mackenzie nodded, and Grace took it as a prompt to continue. "Then, I will bring you both together and work with you to find a solution that you can both live with."

"So, Ashton doesn't want to be my lawyer?" Mackenzie jetted her chin out stubbornly.

"It's more complicated than that."

Mackenzie let out an exasperated sigh before Grace

attempted to present her boss' position in the best light possible.

"I understand Mr. Green has known you and your brother since you were kids, right?"

"Yep."

"So, you would feel very betrayed if he decided to represent your brother in a suit against you, wouldn't you?"

"Damned right I would!"

"Well, you can imagine that your brother would probably feel the same way."

"I guess," Mackenzie conceded.

"That's why no one in the firm will represent you or Gunner. What we can do, however, is work with you to organize a mediation."

"And you would be the one I would work with?"

"Yes. I have been trained to do so, and I'm actually good at it. I think it stems from my deep dislike of conflicts."

"A lawyer who hates conflicts?" Mackenzie laughed. "That's a first."

"Wait, don't get me wrong, I still like a good fight, but I prefer a constructive discussion."

"Okay, I'll bite." Mackenzie set her file aside. "I'll hire you as a mediator. When can you start?"

"As soon as I get a green light from your brother."

The smile vanished from Mackenzie's face. "Good luck with that. He doesn't even pick up my calls anymore, so I don't see how you'll make him agree to sit in the same room with me."

"Why don't you let me worry about that?" Grace offered her best put-them-at-ease smile. "I'm actually meeting with him very soon, and if he agrees, I will start working on your case at once. I understand you're only going to be in town for a few days, right?"

"Oh no, I'm not staying in town," Mackenzie waved away the very concept of remaining in Elm Ridge with a gesture of her hand. "I've taken a room at the Marriott in Lexington, and I can stay until the end of the week. After that, I'll have to go back and get the kids ready for camp."

"I will call you there as soon as I have some news." Grace pushed to her feet, accompanied Mackenzie to the door, and then returned to her office where her boss was waiting for her pacing.

"How did it go?" Ashton Green asked as soon as she entered the room.

"She's in," Grace told him.

"Okay, that's perfect."

"I'm meeting with Gunner later today."

"Then it's practically a done deal."

"Really?"

"Oh, for sure." Ashton smiled at Grace's surprised expression. "I didn't want to tell you that before you talked her into it, but she's the most difficult one of the two. If you sold Mackenzie, you should have no trouble wrapping Gunner around your little finger." Ashton looked at his watch. "Got to run. Let me know how it goes."

As Ashton rushed away, Gloria walked by in the hallway and looked through Grace's open door. "Wanna do lunch?"

"Absolutely."

Grace had a couple of hours before her scheduled meeting with Gunner Cox.

Crossing the street, Grace and Gloria walked into the Quarter Horse Café, the go-to place for the people of the firm. Located between the bank and The Best Little Hair House salon, the lunch spot was always busy.

They both ordered a salad, and as soon as the waitress left, Gloria leaned over to ask, "So Colton, hey, of all the Green boys you met at the party, he's the one you fancy?" Grace frowned at her, and Gloria laughed. "There's one thing you need to understand about small towns. People talk. They talk a lot." She raised a defensive hand as she continued. "They don't mean any harm. On the contrary, they think it's their sacred duty to share any information they were lucky enough to gather."

Grace laughed. People were people, and a small village was not that much different from a big law firm.

Except that in a big law firm people gossiped because knowledge was power, and if you could demonstrate to others that you knew more than they did, you climbed higher up the totem pole.

"I think I liked them all," Grace said. "All five of them!"

"They are six actually."

"I guess I missed one then."

Gloria shook her head, and her smile vanished for an instant. "No, you didn't. The one you've yet to meet is Weston. He should be coming back home soon. His tour of duty will end this summer, but it's neither here or there...." She smiled again. "I hear Colton's the one you spoke to the most at last week's barbecue, and then Friday night you two looked pretty chummy when you danced..." She stopped abruptly, looking straight over Grace's shoulder. "And talk about the devil..."

Turning around, Grace could see Colton Green walking in with another man.

"That's Gunner Cox," Gloria whispered. "He and Colton go way back. They've been best buddies ever since kindergarten."

"Oh, I see."

What Grace saw was one more reason to keep her distance from Colton.

CHAPTER 8

COLTON

"There's no way I'm letting you go by yourself to that meeting," Colton told Gunner as they paid the check.

"Oh, come on," Gunner protested. "If the woman I saw walk out of here with Gloria is really the one I'm going to be meeting with, I'm pretty sure I'm safe."

Colton shook his head in despair. Gunner was great when it came to horses and managing his farm, but for the rest, he was as gullible as they came. His Uncle Ashton knew that, and that's one of the reasons Colton was so mad at him for taking Mackenzie's side. Of course, he hadn't said anything during the Sunday party because it was not the right place to do so, but for sure today Colton would get to the bottom of it.

A minute later, they reached Green and Partners, early for Gunner's appointment with Grace. It was perfect. Colton wanted a moment to talk with Ashton and put an end to the situation before it got out of hand. As soon as the receptionist confirmed that, of course, his uncle had the time to see him right away, he abandoned Gunner in the waiting room and found his way to the main partner's office.

As usual, the place looked like a mess. Files were piled up everywhere. How the man and his assistant managed to find anything, Colton didn't know. Yet, he wasn't there to question his uncle's methods. His filing method seemed strange to him, but his uncle Ashton had been running a very successful practice for thirty years, so there was no reason to attempt to fix something that wasn't broken.

"Colton, what a delightful surprise." Ashton walked around the desk to give him a hug. "What can I do for you?"

They both sat on the visitor's side of the immense desk, the only area clear of piles of paper, and Colton came right out with it. "I came here with Gunner."

Ashton nodded but didn't comment.

"And I really don't understand why, if you felt like you could favor one of the twins, you decided to favor Mackenzie. It isn't like you at all."

Ashton looked thoughtfully at his nephew, rubbed his temples, and seemed to hesitate for an instant. "You realize you're overstepping?"

Colton shrugged. He sort of was, but then again, Gunner was a pushover, and what sort of friend would he be if he didn't look out for him?

"You also must realize that I can't possibly tell you anything about this case. No matter how close Gunner and you are, there are ethical rules that I will not ignore."

"And what if Gunner wants me by his side?" Colton clenched his fists, ready for a verbal battle.

"That would be a different matter entirely since he has the right to be accompanied by whomever he wants to," Ashton answered, surprising him. "If Gunner wants you to sit in the meeting he's about to have with Grace, you could... *but* you need to think hard about the message you're sending him if you do so."

"What do you mean?"

"Well, up to now you've been nothing but a good friend staying by his side as he gets ready for what he expects to be a difficult meeting."

Colton tilted his head in agreement.

"But if you walk in there with him, what sort of message do you think you'll be sending?" Ashton let a moment pass to let Colton think about it.

The question called forth childhood images into the younger man's mind—Gunner being called all sorts of nasty names by his father, or Gunner coming to school with two shiners and Mackenzie confiding that he got beat up while getting in their dad's way to protect her or their mother. Being called a *good for nothing scum of the earth* on a regular basis didn't help a boy build up his self-confidence. Gunner only started standing on his own two feet after his father's passing, when he had no choice but step up and take over the management of the farm.

"Maybe I'll just hang out in the waiting room for a bit then," Colton said.

"Or maybe you'll trust me and offer to meet him for dinner. It could take a while."

"You think?"

"I sure hope so."

"Fine, I'll let you get back to work then." Colton stood up and worked his way out through the paper maze. At the door, he turned around and said, "Thank you."

"Any time, Colton. Anytime."

A few seconds later, Colton reached the waiting room, just in time to watch Grace greet Gunner. She looked stunning in her lawyer's suit, her hair pulled back like it had been the first time they had met. Good. Strangely, he felt happy she wore it like this in the office; it made her look a bit severe. The softer side of her, the one that showed when she let her hair down, should be reserved for a more intimate setting.

Wow, Colton had no idea where that was coming from. It wasn't as if he had any reason to have a say about how she lived her life.

"Hello, Grace," he said, startling her a bit.

"Oh, hello Colton. I didn't know you were here."

"You two know each other?" Gunner eyes darted between Grace and Colton.

"We have met a couple of times," Grace answered.

"What she means is that we're still in the getting-to-know-each-another phase," Colton explained. "When you told me about this meeting with a new member of the firm, I thought that it might be with Grace."

"So, that's why you wanted to come along," Gunner whispered.

Colton heard the disappointment in his voice. The man was so used to being betrayed. Colton hoped Gunner didn't believe he'd tagged along for ulterior motives. "Of course not! Come on, Gunner, you know better than that. I'm here because I've got your back."

Gunner shrugged, "Yeah, whatever."

"Do you want me to wait for you here, or should we meet up at your place later tonight?" Colton asked.

"If I may," Grace cut in before Gunner had a chance to answer. "I want to say two things. The first one is that I'm not the enemy here. Gunner doesn't need any protection from me. The second is that this could take a while so maybe…"

"Go," Gunner said. "I'll call you when I get out."

"Fine." Turning to Grace, Colton sternly declared, "You take good care of my friend now, you hear?"

Grace smiled and shooed him away. "I'm pretty sure Mr. Cox can hold his own."

Well, Colton was not. She could have him under her spell in a minute. And that worried him.

Yes, it probably worried him more than it should.

CHAPTER 9

GRACE

"Please call me Gunner." He followed her into the small conference room where Grace had met with his sister a few hours ago.

"I will if you call me Grace." She shut the door behind them.

He looked around suspiciously. "What kind of conference room is this?"

"It's one Ashton Green created for meetings such as this one."

Gunner laughed and looked at her sideways. She could see the wheels turning. Heaven knew what he was thinking. "Shall we sit?"

"Sure." He took a seat on the edge of a sofa. "I'm curious as to what this is about. I mean, I know it's about the estate, but..."

Grace took a seat and began her well-practiced explanation. "Have you heard of ADR?"

"Sort of," he answered. "I did look it up after I received your letter and researched you."

"Good."

"But I'm not sure how this concerns me."

"Let me explain then. Mackenzie Cox reached out to Mr. Green."

The very sound of his sister's name was enough to make him cringe and look in the direction of the door.

"Now hear me out, please," Grace raised a hand. "Mr. Green has refused to represent her in a suit against you."

Gunner looked at her again. "So, he didn't turn his back on me?"

"No, but he didn't want to turn his back on your sister either."

Gunner seemed puzzled. He was locked in a binary mode. What Grace needed was to show him it was possible to be in his corner without being against his sister and vice versa.

"So, what Mr. Green is proposing is a mediation."

"What the heck is that?"

"A possibility for you and your sister to come to an understanding." Grace hoped he was going to be as agreeable as Ashton had thought he would.

Gunner adopted a more comfortable position on the sofa and waited for Grace to continue.

She gave him a brief overview of the way the process worked and stressed that the firm would be doing it pro bono. "Do you want to think about it for a bit, or can we get started right away?"

"So, you say Ashton won't charge us for your time?" Gunner seemed surprised.

"Yes, it is my understanding that Mr. Green has genuine affection for the two of you and believes this should be resolved outside a courthouse."

"Then, I guess I don't have anything to lose, do I?"

"Simply a few hours of your time."

"Fine, let's do this." Gunner moved to the edge of his seat, his entire body language changing. Leery before, now like a thoroughbred ready to bolt at the sound of the starting gun, he was ready for the race.

"I was hoping you would say that." Grace picked up a pad and pen from a side table. "Why don't you start by telling me how your sister and you became estranged."

"Oh, that's easy. She ran. The day she turned eighteen, she left and never looked back." He sighed and rubbed his face. "That's it."

Grace heard so much anger and so much pain that her heart went out to him. "She left without telling you she would?"

Gunner shook his head adamantly. "No, it wasn't like that. She asked me to go with her, but I couldn't."

"Why not?" Grace asked gently. No judgment there, just curiosity.

"Well, you know..."

"No. I don't."

"You mean Ashton didn't tell you about our dad?"

"No, Mr. Green did his best not to influence me in any way. He only gave me bare-bones information about Mackenzie and you. I know you're twins because you have the same birthdate, and I know your father passed away shortly after you turned nineteen and your mother survived until early May of this year. I understand she left you and your sister a ranch, and you both could possibly use some help to liquidate the estate."

"Oh, I see." Some of his fire seemed to fizzle in his eyes.

"So, what is it I should know about your father?"

"That he was always rough, but he was also a decent enough sort of man. That is, until his injury," Gunner stared at the tip of his boots. "After that, he changed."

Men and their understatements. From the look on

Gunner's face, Grace surmised that the change was serious in nature. "Is this change the reason your sister decided to leave?"

He nodded.

"And you refused to go with her because..."

"Someone had to stay home." The fire in his eyes returned. He stared at Grace hard, as if defying her to push him further.

Understanding that he would shut down if she kept on probing, she picked a different angle. "Since he passed, you've been running the ranch?"

"That I have," he answered proudly. "Brought it back from the dead, so to speak."

"Congratulations. Now, I don't know much about ranch management, but I think it's safe to assume that this is no small feat and that you worked really hard to do so."

"You bet, I did." He didn't elaborate, but by the way he looked at her, Grace knew he was thinking giving up half the ranch would be unfair.

And it would. This situation was a new version of the prodigal son. Gunner stayed home, worked hard, and saved the family ranch from a possible bankruptcy, while Mackenzie ran away. Now, because the mother had passed without writing a will, she stood to inherit half of something that wouldn't be there without Gunner.

Grace made him talk about his work, and he warmed up. His passion for horses was communicative, and it was clear he had big plans for the place—big plans which were threatened by his sister's return. When he'd relaxed enough, Grace probed again. "I have a delicate question for you."

"Figures." He laughed sadly. "For a moment, I almost forgot why I was here."

"You don't have to answer right now. Actually, I would rather you take some time to think about it for a bit."

He tilted his head and waited for the question.

"If it were entirely up to you," Grace said very slowly, looking into his eyes, "if anything at all, what do you think Mackenzie should get?"

He rolled his lips inward and turned his gaze away.

Grace gave him a good minute of small talk to digest the question. It was time to put an end to their meeting. "Maybe we've done enough for today. What would you say about meeting again soon to discuss this further?"

"I would like that very much."

Grace then accompanied him back to the reception area.

Just as he was about to walk out, he turned around and asked softly, "Will Mackenzie be here next time?"

The question was loaded with emotion, but Grace couldn't tell if it was hope or dread.

"Next time, it will be entirely up to you," she reassured him. "But sooner or later, it would be good if you could talk face-to-face."

Standing tall, hands in his pockets, he nodded and walked away.

Grace closed the door and leaned against it for a bit.

Mediation was often rewarding, but it was also emotionally draining. On days like today, she wished she had someone to go home to and share a drink.

Yes, a glass of a wine would be nice.

Or maybe she could learn to like Bourbon.

CHAPTER 10

COLTON

For two days Colton hadn't been able to get the New York lawyer out of his mind. He looked at his watch again. It was one o'clock, and he was beginning to think that he'd wasted his time. This crazy woman would not stop for a lunch break today. Five more minutes.

He was still pacing in the bookstore when Gloria sent him a text. *Grace is on her way out.* Colton left the shop just as Grace exited from the adjacent office building. He caught up with her before she had a chance to cross the street.

"Hello, Grace."

Surprised, she jumped a step back. "Oh, Colton."

"Sorry, didn't mean to startle you. On your way to lunch?"

"Well, uh…"

"Would you like some company?"

"Maybe another day. I was just about to go pick up a sandwich to eat at my desk."

"Oh," Colton put on what Sophia called his beaten puppy look. "Since we never had a chance for a proper goodbye the other night, I thought I could make it up to you with a nice lunch."

Grace tilted her head and stared hard. "Colton Green, were you on your way to see me?"

"Not exactly." He chuckled. "I've sort of been waiting in the bookstore for you to go to lunch forever."

"Oh, well …" Color filled her cheeks.

"Surely you could spare a few minutes for a starving man who doesn't want to eat alone."

"Well, if you put it that way, I guess. Maybe we could grab a quick bite and eat out here." She pointed towards the town square.

"Sounds good to me."

They both ordered Hot Browns to go from the Quarter Horse Café and five minutes later found a shady bench to share.

"What were you really waiting for?" she asked before taking a bite of her sandwich.

"I actually wanted to apologize."

"Apologize, whatever for?"

"Thinking the worst of you." Colton looked into her eyes.

She frowned and chewed in silence.

"I had this preconceived notion about you."

"Because?"

"You're a city girl and a lawyer."

"I guess those are two cardinal sins," she raised her brows at him.

"Well, I couldn't possibly hold the city girl thing against you," he conceded. "After all, we don't choose where we're born and raised."

"So, you gave me extenuating circumstances for that first offense, how generous of you." She skewered him with a court-room glare.

This wasn't going quite the way he'd hoped it would. "But you did decide to become a lawyer."

"I actually worked very hard to make it happen."

Suddenly, he wanted to know why she'd had to work so hard. That would be a conversation for another day, after he'd dug himself out of his current hole. "What I mean is, before you, I always thought attorneys were necessary evils at best."

"Even your uncle Ashton?" Her eyebrow shot up high again.

"Ashton is different, you know. He's family."

Her eyes twinkled with restrained humor. "I see."

"So, when I found out you were going to meet with Gunner, I imagined the worst."

"Hmm..." She raised her hand to stop him and chewed a little faster.

Colton wanted to reassure her right away, make her understand he was not there to question what she was doing or ask her to violate any confidence. "Now, I realize you can't talk to me about the case, but I don't think there's a rule that prohibits you from listening to what I have to say, right?"

"Maybe not, but it would still be better if we didn't talk about it at all."

"Agreed, but I still want to say that the talks you've had with Gunner have done him a world of good. You've forced him to face the demons that were eating him up, and for that, I am very grateful."

The twinkle in her gaze brightened. "I'm happy to know that I have somehow redeemed my profession in your eyes."

"The jury is still out on your profession, but the verdict has been rendered for you."

"So, I'm no longer just a necessary evil?"

Colton shook his head. "Nope, you're a kind and generous human being, and that means a lot around here."

She blushed a little and looked away.

"It also means the world to me. So much that I really want

to get to know you better. Would you go out with me on Saturday night?"

Grace hesitated. "I'm not sure. Willow and I had talked about going to the movies. I'm glad she's here for at least part of the summer."

Colton loved the way her face lit up when she was genuinely happy. Willow was a nice kid. But he also noticed the way Grace's new friend looked at one of his brothers. He wasn't even sure Sophia had noticed either. He hoped Willow wasn't in for too big of a let down.

They continued to eat their lunch in silence for a bit.

"Having lunch here is delightful." Grace looked in direction of the main street. "It's a refreshing change from the constant hum of the restaurant."

"Maybe we could have another outdoor dinner before taking in a movie on Saturday?"

Grace stared in the distance as if she hadn't heard him.

"Is there a reason why you wouldn't want to spend some time with me?"

Grace turned around to face him and smiled. "Well, not really. Except that you're my boss's nephew and the best friend of a client, and..."

Colton cut her short. "Grace you're not in New York anymore. This is Elm Ridge, Kentucky. We're a very small community with large families and strong ties. Everyone is related one way or another to everyone else. I may have over fifty direct blood relatives just in the county, and triple that if you look in the entire state."

Grace looked away again as she processed this information.

"And then because we only have one high school, by the time we're ready to move to college, we're friends or foes with most of the kids in our age range, give or take a few years."

"I see." That seemed to be Grace's default answer when she didn't know what else to say.

"In other words, it's going to be very lonely for you if you keep at arm's length everyone who is related or friendly with people you work with or for. Unless you have another reason for not wanting to go out with me on Saturday. Are we on?"

Grace seemed to think very hard about it but didn't object.

"Good, then it's settled," Colton said, rolling up their sandwich wrappings in a ball. "I'll come pick you up at your place at what? Six thirty?"

"Six thirty is fine," she answered.

"See you then." He rushed away before she had a chance to change her mind.

CHAPTER 11

GRACE

Colton walked away at a brisk pace. Grace watched him tilt his head at a few people who crossed his path in the town square and then stop to speak to an elderly lady who patted his arms as if he were a kitten. They hugged and he continued on. She hadn't thought to ask if he had an office in town. For some reason, she figured he would work out of the manufacturing facility.

Grace leisurely returned to the firm, basking in the spring warmth. It had barely been one month, but she thought she was adapting to the Elm Ridge rhythm. Life was so different here.

When she arrived at the office, Kate, the receptionist, greeted her with a smile.

"Your two o'clock is here," she said, tilting her head towards the waiting room glass doors.

And indeed, Mackenzie had arrived early. She was fiddling with her phone looking preoccupied. Grace pushed the door open and said, "I'm so happy you could make it. Do you want to start early, or do you need to finish what you're doing?"

She shook her head and dropped the phone in her bag.

"I'm all yours. Let's get this over with," she answered with a clipped tone.

Grace didn't know what was eating her up, but clearly, she was not in as mellow a mood as the last time.

"Did you meet with my brother?" she asked as they made their way to the cozy conference room.

"Yes, I did, and he agreed to give mediation a try."

"So, he'd rather talk to a total stranger than to his twin, hey." There was so much bitterness in Mackenzie's voice that there was no denying her pain. "Oh, I probably shouldn't have said that out loud, should I? I'm sorry, I didn't mean to offend you."

"No offense taken," Grace reassured her. "Oftentimes it's easier to speak to strangers."

They settled on their respective sofas and then Grace asked her to tell her version of the story.

"Since you spoke to Gunner already, he must have told you about our father."

"What do you think he told me?"

"I'm sure he made all sort of excuses for him before he came around to admitting he was..." she looked for the appropriate word her brother could have used and came up with "...difficult."

Grace smiled and conceded that most men do have a way of going for understatements rather than talk openly about situations that made them uncomfortable.

"Well the truth is, he was a mean, self-centered, abusive monster," Mackenzie declared.

With a nod, Grace encouraged her to continue.

"I petitioned for emancipation when I turned seventeen, but dear Daddy got the judge to deny my request. After that, I tried running away a few times, but he always managed to find me." She shuddered and braced herself. "So, I bided my time, and on the day we turned eighteen, I was packed and ready to go."

"Gunner said you asked him to go with you," Grace chimed in softly.

"I didn't ask, I begged! I was terrified to go away on my own, but he wouldn't run with me. Couldn't leave our mother alone, he said. The woman couldn't be bothered to protect us, but of course, he had to protect her." She shook her head as if to say that it was an absurd answer. "So, even though the world looked like a big scary place, I figured it had to be better than our home. I left without him."

"And you never looked back?"

"I had to cut all ties. I had so much anger that I didn't even want to hear about anyone in Elm Ridge. Now, of course, in hindsight I realize I could have handled things differently. Doctor Nayar offered to help. She suspected my injuries were not all accidental, but I told her what a klutz I was and shut her down. And since Dad always drove Mom to see his retired family doctor, Doctor Nayar never got a chance to confirm her suspicions."

"What about Gunner?" Grace asked.

"The stable staff took care of him…"

Grace now had a better picture of the situation. Big town, small town, it was all the same. When the persecutor is smart enough, the victims feel too much shame to speak up.

The two women remained silent for a bit until Grace prompted Mackenzie to continue.

"But then your father passed, and it was just your mother and Gunner."

"When that happened, I was too busy with my own life to look back. I only found out about it several years later when I ran into one of the Green sisters in Miami. It was spring break. At the time, I thought Audrey had had way too much to drink to remember our encounter, but it turns out I was wrong. She told Ashton, and he's the one who reached out to me when Mom passed."

Another moment of silence. Grace knew she had to let Mackenzie tell the story at her own pace.

"I asked if Mom had left everything to Gunner, and he said that as far as he knew, she had never written a will. So, I looked it up online and found out that I stand to inherit half of everything, and that's why I came back."

"To claim your half?"

Mackenzie looked at Grace as if she'd ask the craziest question, and then her hand flew to her mouth.

"Oh, my Lord, is that what everyone thinks? Ashton thought I wanted to hire him to sue my brother and get half of the estate? Is this what Gunner thinks too?"

"I can't tell you what Gunner thinks, but I can tell you I assumed you came back to liquidate the estate. Not knowing you, I didn't presume further about your intentions. This is why I'm asking."

Mackenzie breathed a heavy sigh of relief.

"Okay, so, let's be clear. Now, I think it should all go to Gunner 'cause he's the one attached to the land."

"You say *now*. Does that mean initially you considered asking for something?"

Mackenzie waved Grace's question away with a dismissive gesture that the attorney decided to ignore.

"Please tell me?"

Mackenzie hesitated and then gave in. "Before I realized how angry Gunner still was at me for leaving, I was going to ask for the shack by the lake."

Now they were getting somewhere.

"Tell me about it."

"It's really not much more than an old barn, but Gunner

and I used to hide out there when we were kids. It was our safe place. Somewhere we could spend time without fear of being interrupted by our father. See, he was a regular mosquito magnet and was eaten alive any time he came too close."

The smile on her face told of happy memories—memories obviously shared with her brother.

"I've always had this crazy dream of bringing my kids over there in the summer. And then I imagined I could move back to Elm Ridge for good and that Gunner would help me raise them. It would be good for them to have a man in their lives, and it would also give him an opportunity to figure out he could be good with kids, to reassure him and make him see that if he ever becomes a father, he will not be like our dad."

She wiped the corner of her eye and shrugged.

"Would you be ready to explain this to him in person?" Grace asked.

"In person?" Mackenzie repeated. "But he won't pick up my calls, so ..."

"I told him you were going back home at the end of the week, and he's agreed to a meeting on Friday, preferably in the evening."

"And you work on Friday evenings?"

"Yeah, for very special cases, I do."

Especially the ones with a happy ending.

But Grace didn't say it for fear of jinxing herself.

CHAPTER 12

COLTON

Gunner looked into the glass the waitress brought. He was all thoughtful, which was not like him.

"I really like this woman," he whispered.

"The waitress?" Colton asked, turning his head around to give her another look.

Gunner laughed.

"Nah, I mean Grace Baker!"

"Oh!"

"Don't look so annoyed with me. I don't like her like that," Gunner explained with a knowing smile.

Now, what is he talking about?

"You don't like her like what?"

"I like that she's smart and in control and all that. I really do, 'cause it makes me believe she'll be able to find a solution for Mackenzie and me. So, I like her a lot—but not like you do."

Colton frowned, wondering where this was coming from.

"Basically, what I'm saying is that a woman like that would scare the crap out of me, but I can see why you like her," Gunner added.

For a second, Colton considered the possibility of denying the attraction he felt for Grace, and then thought better of it. He didn't want to lie to Gunner. He never had. Gunner was like family to him. He had, on occasion, sugarcoated the truth a bit, but no, he had never lied to him.

"And what I've seen of her makes me think she'd be good for you."

Now that was interesting. "Really?"

"Yeah." Gunner ran his finger around the edge of his glass and looked up to his friend. "You and your temper, you need a strong woman, one who can stand up to you, and that Grace, she seems to have enough of a backbone to do that."

Colton nodded because even if he didn't know her that well yet, he was certain she was strong-willed. There was no denying Gunner was right. He did like a woman who could stand up to him and on her own two feet.

"She's smart." Gunner said *smart* as if it was a bad thing.

His lack of self-confidence was no secret to Colton. Yes, Gunner thought he would be unable to deal with a smart woman. He thought he didn't deserve to be with one. He feared that if he did, sooner or later, she would realize what an idiot he was and leave.

Gunner may not have been the shrewdest person around, but he had demonstrated to Colton and to the world, time and time again, that he was no dummy. After all, he had singlehandedly brought back the family ranch from the dead and turned it into a profitable enterprise. That was quite an accomplishment. Yet, he didn't see himself as a good rancher. His father had done such a number on him that he would probably spend the rest of his life second guessing himself.

Colton wished there was a way he could undo the damage, but he had no clue where to start. One thing he knew for sure though was that what he lacked in brains, Gunner compensated for with courage and determination. He was a good person, and he would make some lucky woman a fabulous husband, if only he would give himself a chance.

"I'll grant you that Grace can be a bit intimidating," Colton agreed.

"Yep. Most smart women are." Gunner looked away dreamily, and Colton knew where his mind had gone.

Since sixth grade, he'd had a thing for Audrey. Even though she was one year younger than the twins, Audrey and Mackenzie were close friends. They had done the ballet thing together, and since old man Cox couldn't be bothered to pay any attention to what his daughter was doing, it was Gunner who made sure Mackenzie wouldn't have to walk back home alone on practice and rehearsal nights.

Gunner's expression lightened. "Did I mention I'm gonna be teaching at the camp for Jaxon this summer."

"You are?"

"Jaxon decided it would do the kids good to get some ethology notions."

"That's the natural behavior stuff, right?" Colton did ride, everyone in the family did, and he sort of enjoyed it, but that was it. He was the only Green who hadn't been bitten by the horse bug. Still, he knew what to do around a stable and could take care of horses if he had to. It was just a thing he knew how to do, like driving, but it wasn't a passion.

"Yes, it's a more humane way to work with horses," Gunner explained. "It's challenging at times, but when you do get through, you have this most amazing relationship with the animal."

Gunner shone when he talked about horses.

"You see it's all about building trust..."

Colton tuned out Gunner's horse related rambling and wondered if everything in life didn't revolve around trust.

Trust didn't come naturally for him.

Suspicion was his default attitude with everyone else but his closest family. He trusted his parents blindly. They had demonstrated that they would always be there for him. He trusted his brothers and his sister, who never questioned he was one of them. He guessed he trusted Gunner as well. At least, he knew his friend would never willingly do anything to harm him.

But that was it.

No matter how hard he tried, Colton remained suspicious of the rest of the world.

Sometimes he imagined he was making progress on that front, but now that he thought about it, there was no denying he was lying to himself. His knee-jerk reaction had been to suspect Ashton of betraying Gunner when he should have given his uncle the benefit of the doubt. He hadn't. He had imagined the worst instantly.

The same held true for Grace.

He liked her, yet he barely knew her.

Gunner was right, it was all about building trust.

Somehow, Colton hoped he would learn to trust Grace.

CHAPTER 13

GRACE

Grace paced in the reception area waiting for Mackenzie. She had asked her to come at six to whisk her away in the conference room before her brother arrived. She'd told him to come at six thirty, and she'd bet on his arriving in advance.

Their reunion needed to be in a controlled environment and not a chance encounter in the waiting room where they would be feeling trapped and uncomfortable.

In some cases, Grace had gone as far as baking cookies and warming them up in the conference room. There was something about the smell of melted chocolate that soothed people. Real estate agents knew all about this. But she didn't chance it in this case. From what she had gathered, childhood memories were the last thing she wanted to summon right now. Even if it was the two of them against their father.

Mackenzie arrived at six on the dot. She looked frazzled.

"Is everything okay?" Grace asked, steering her directly toward the back.

"Do I look that bad?" she answered with a sad smile.

"No, not bad. Just tense."

She was a handsome woman struggling to hold herself together. She was gracious under pressure.

"That I am, but it's not only this," Mackenzie said. "I had a major work crisis yesterday and it kept me up all night."

"Did you fix it?"

"Yeah, it's going to be all right. It's just that some clients are regular prima donnas, and—" She took position on one sofa and looked up at Grace. "But you must know all about that, right?"

"Oh, don't get me started!"

Both women laughed.

Mackenzie had yet to mention what sort of business she was in, but Grace guessed a service one. Also, if she were to judge by her appearance, Grace would have said she was doing well. Very well actually. The clothes were nondescript chain store brands, stuff that anyone could afford, but the handbag and the shoes told a different story. They were exquisite leather. The bag alone would pay for six months of Grace's mortgage, which reminded her, she needed to go online to make sure Sam hadn't forgotten to pay theirs.

Concentrate, Grace, concentrate.

"Are you ready? Your brother should be here any minute, and I'll bring him over."

She nodded, but her entire body was stiff as a board.

"It's going to be all right," Grace assured her. She didn't have to put on airs for her. She truly believed they were going to find an agreement. They didn't have any conflicting interests, really, they didn't. What they had was difficulty communicating, and Grace knew how to help with that sort of issue. Forced proximity and a stern hand was often all it took.

"Okay," Mackenzie said with a warmer smile. "Go get him. I promise not to run."

Grace retraced her steps to the waiting room to find

Gunner pacing in front of the reception desk like a lion in a cage.

"Is she here?" he asked the second he saw her.

"Yes, and she's about as anxious as you are," Grace told him.

A voice behind her startled her. "Well she should be!"

Colton's voice. She hadn't seen him standing in the corner of the room. Gunner frowned at him, and Colton raised both hands in surrender.

"I won't say another word," Colton stated, opening the door. "Well, except hello, Grace, you look lovely today."

"Well thank you, Colton." She turned to Gunner and asked, "Shall we go?"

He mumbled something incomprehensible and threw an awkward glance in the direction of his friend.

"You're going to be fine," Colton said. "I know I'm leaving you in good hands."

The door closed behind him. It was just the receptionist, ready to jump out the door to go home, Gunner, and Grace.

"Let's do this," he said, marching down the hall with the enthusiasm of a prisoner walking toward a firing squad.

When he reached the door, he took a step back to let Grace open it. When she did, he remained frozen at the doorstep but managed to say with a choked voice, "Mackenzie."

His sister stood and took a step forward. "Gunner." She controlled her emotions better, but her eyes were filled with tears. She blinked and made them disappear. "I'm so happy you're here."

Gunner took a timid step inside the room and hesitated.

What did one do with a sibling one hadn't seen in over ten years? A greeting less distant than a handshake but not as familiar as a hug had yet to be invented for such an occasion.

"Why don't you sit here?" Grace suggested to Gunner, pointing to the small empty sofa so he could face his sister.

"What about you?" he asked.

"I will stand for now, and then, I have this chair." Grace pointed to a folding chair right behind the door.

Mackenzie and Gunner sat on their opposite sofas, and both stared at their hands as if they were fascinating creatures that required all their attention. The resemblance in mannerism was striking. Also, there were physical similarities that Grace hadn't noticed before—same color hair, same eyes, same nose. That's why she had thought of Mackenzie as a *handsome* woman. But one thing was for sure, he wasn't a pretty boy. He was a handsome and manly one.

"I think the best way to start, if you both agree, is for Mackenzie to tell you the reason for her visit," Grace said.

"What's the point?" Gunner snarled. "We all know why she's here."

"See, what did I tell you?" Mackenzie asked Grace. "There's no talking to him. He's stubborn as a mule."

"Would you two please stop it this instant!"

Her best school teacher voice worked. The two wildcats ready to pounce on each other fell back into their seats and mumbled matching apologies.

"I said that Mackenzie would explain why she came and," Grace looked sternly at Gunner, "when she's done, it will be your turn to express yourself."

Mackenzie glanced in Grace's direction, and she signaled that she had the floor.

"I came here so we could deal with the estate," she started.

Gunner was on the edge of his seat again and opened his mouth, but one look in Grace's direction and he closed it without making a sound. Good.

"I thought it would be easier if I came and you didn't need

to track me down."

He nodded and still refrained from saying anything.

"So, the reason I came is to make it easy on you," she said.

He rolled his eyes at her. That was the last straw for her. She stood.

"You really don't get it do you?" she asked but didn't wait for an answer. "I don't want anything. You can keep it all and…" Her eyes were full of tears again, but this time she didn't bother to try to hide them as she looked back at Grace. "Just draw up the papers, and I'll sign whatever you need me to sign so he never has to hear about me again."

Grace took a step back and placed herself against the door to block Mackenzie's exit, but she didn't need to. Gunner had jumped up and taken his sister in his arms.

"Don't cry, Mackenzie," he whispered in her ear. "You know I can't stand to see you cry."

He petted her hair and squeezed her so hard Grace feared for a minute Mackenzie was going to break. She didn't and clung back on to him.

"I've missed you," she said. "I've missed you so darn much."

Grace let them stand like that for a bit and looked away when Gunner wiped a runaway tear from a corner of one eye.

"Why don't we sit down?" Grace suggested speaking very softly.

They both nodded, and when Gunner acted as if he was going back to the opposite sofa, his sister took his hand and made him sit next to her.

Good, that gave Grace a chance to occupy the empty seat and face them both.

"So, Gunner," Grace said, "now that Mackenzie has explained why she came here, is there something you would like to tell her?"

"What do you mean you want nothing?" he asked. "This land isn't good enough for you anymore?"

For a second Grace thought Gunner was angry, but then she understood he was sad and hurt. Talk about a change of attitude!

"Actually," Grace spoke up, "there is one thing your sister would very much like as her share of the estate."

Gunner's eyes darted between his sister and Grace as if he was not sure who he should ask what it was his twin wanted. Grace tilted her head to indicate that he should be asking his sister.

"So come on," he growled. "Tell me."

"I thought maybe you'd let me have the shack," she whispered.

"The shack?" he repeated, making it sound like a foreign word. A hint of a smile appeared at the corner of his mouth when he asked, "The shack by the lake?"

She nodded, and he laughed, a big belly laugh, like it was the funniest joke ever.

"That's the one thing you can't have," he said.

"Oh." All the disappointment in the world was summarized in one syllable.

"You can't have it 'cause I tore it down, Sis," he explained. "I tore it down and burned every last piece of wood into a cinder."

Mackenzie frowned and asked, "Why in heaven's name did you do that?"

"Because I started building on that very spot. I got started with our house, you know, the big house we dreamed of sharing," he said with a breathtaking smile. "I figured if I started building it, maybe you would come home."

And now it was Grace's turn to wipe a runaway tear from the corner of her eye.

CHAPTER 14

COLTON

At six thirty, Colton parked in front of Mrs. Carson's house. The very second he got out of the car, he noticed discreet movement of the curtain by the door. No surprise there. The Carson widow probably did not get many visitors since her son had left. According to Colton's mother, that woman had never been a very social creature, but still, Colton felt for her. It had to be lonely for her with no family around.

Colton waved at the form behind the curtain and called out, "Good evening, Mrs. Carson."

A few seconds later, the door opened and the old lady squinted out at him.

"I'm Colton Green," he told her. "Julia and Landon's second son."

She tilted her head and snorted, "You don't need to pretend with me. I know who you are."

Colton then understood what his mother was hinting at when she had mumbled something about her being alone and reaping what she sowed.

Unwilling to give her the satisfaction of seeing if her mean words got to him or not, Colton wore his warmest smile and simply said, "It was nice seeing you again."

Colton turned his back to her and directed his steps toward the eastern side of the house. Gloria had told him Grace's place had its own door.

The old witch slammed her door shut before Colton reached the corner of her home. Good riddance!

A knock on the door, and Grace opened in a second.

"Hey," she said, a little out of breath.

"Good evening," he answered, taking in how lovely she looked.

She shook her black mane to one side of her neck, ran her eyes from the tip of his boots to his face, and laughed.

"Sorry," she said as soon as she noticed Colton's puzzled expression. "See, you hadn't said where we were going, so I didn't know how to dress, and now I see I got lucky."

It was Colton's turn to scan her from head to toe to discover she'd dressed just like him—a crisp white shirt, jeans, and boots. A silk scarf gave her overall appearance a classier look though.

"This is perfect for where we're going," Colton told her.

"Let me get my bag, and I'll be right with you," she said as she vanished inside, leaving the door open behind her.

Since she hadn't invited him in, he remained at the doorstep, but curiosity got the best of him. Colton peeked inside to see what her furnished rental looked like. It was sparse, to say the least. The large room boasted, on one side, a battered sofa facing a mantelpiece. Next to it, there was one of those all-in-one fridge-stovetop-sink units, as well as a small square table with a single chair. On the other side of the room was a single bed and a door opening on what Colton guessed was a bathroom.

Grace took a sweater from a clothing rack on wheels by

the bed and picked up her handbag from the table. She turned around and grinned.

"Oh, my keys," she said, going to the table to grab a set attached to a keychain bearing the logo of a local gas station.

Colton stepped back to let her close the door, and after she was done, she bent over to pick up a sort of grayish rock from the dirt. She flipped it around revealing a cavity in which she dropped the key.

"See, I have this thing with keys," she said as she put the rock back in its place. "I tend to lose them, so I came up with a solution. I leave my set by the door and don't have to worry about it anymore."

"Does Mrs. Carson know you're doing this?" Colton asked.

"Of course," she answered, following him in direction of his car. "I asked her for permission 'cause, you know, it's her furniture in there."

"And she didn't object, I'm sure," Colton commented. Why would she? Anyone who would be crazy enough to steal her battered furniture would be saving her the cost of hauling it away.

"No, she didn't." She gave him a sheepish smile and whispered, "I think she was delighted about it because it gives her an opportunity to deny it's her who periodically comes snooping around my place."

"What?" Colton was horrified. Hadn't she ever heard of privacy? "And you're okay with that?" he asked, opening the car door for her.

"I never take anything confidential outside the office and, for the rest, my life is pretty much an open book." Grace shrugged. "I figure that if her life is so empty, she needs to look into mine for distraction, I should feel sorry and not angry at her, no?"

Colton mulled this over on the way to his side of the car.

Nah, angry would trump sorry for me, he decided. "This is unacceptable. I'm sure if you told Gloria, she'd be as mad as I am right now. Oh yeah, she would find you another place in an instant."

"You're probably right," Grace agreed thoughtfully.

"But?"

"But it is my understanding that Mrs. Carson really needs the money and, one way or another, I'll be out of there before the end of next month."

Colton quickly took his eyes from the road to look at her. She was staring straight ahead with a happy smile on her face.

"One way or another? What does that mean?"

"Mr. Green said—"

He cut her off. "You don't call him Ashton?"

"No. He's asked me to, but for now, I think it's good to keep some distance with the boss, especially during a trial period."

"So, what did my uncle say?" Colton prompted to get her back on track.

"He said that we would have a discussion before the end of the month, early July at the latest," her voice dropped as she attempted to imitate his uncle's baritone. "We'll decide if we're a good match and all."

Colton laughed because she did a great likeness of him.

With her normal voice she continued. "So, it can go either of two ways, but in both cases, I'll move out of Mrs. Carson's home to find a place of my own. The new place will be in Elm Ridge, if Mr. Green wants me to stay. If he doesn't, then I guess I'll move to another town, wherever someone will hire me."

"You make it sound as if it's entirely up to him," he observed.

"Oh, yes. At this point it is. I'm sold. I love it here!" she said with heartwarming enthusiasm. "The work is challenging, but in a good way, not like it was in New York. I have time to think, and don't feel like I'm always trying to catch up with my own shadow. The other lawyers are cordial, the support staff is fabulous, and so far it's been a positive experience." She sighed and continued. "I realize I'm only talking about work, but that's because it still takes up most of my days. I have yet to develop an active social life, but so far, everyone has been pleasant. Gloria has taken me under her wing, and I think your sister and her bestie like me too, so making new friends is a work in progress."

"And you forgot to talk about me!" Colton said with a sad little boy's voice.

"Now, what should I have said about you?" she asked playfully.

"You tell me!" Colton let a few seconds pass giving her some time to give the subject some consideration and then decided against it. "Don't answer that. Not now. I'll ask you again when I take you back home tonight."

Hopefully, by then she would think that maybe he could be one more reason to stick around his lovely little town.

CHAPTER 15

GRACE

"An open book," he said. "So, what should I know about you?"

Grace laughed. That was a trick question. She started with neutral information, stuff he could find on the internet if he researched her.

"Born and raised in New York City, lived there all my life until I moved here."

"So not a globe trotter," he commented.

"Nope, but I would love to become one, wouldn't you?"

"I would love to travel, but for now, it's not in the cards. Not with Weston away..." He didn't finish his sentence.

"Weston, that's the brother I have yet to meet. The one who's in the military?"

"Yeah, he's also the only one of my siblings who really loves making Bourbon," he said. "So, when he's around he works with me."

"With you and Veronica?"

He smiled when she mentioned her name.

"Yeah, with Veronica and Mom as well," he repeated. "The

business comes from the maternal side of the family. It was started by my great-grandmother."

"Wait, wait," Grace said, doing a quick computation in my head. "Your great-grandmother? That means she got started during prohibition."

Colton laughed and agreed, "Absolutely."

"Oh, you'll have to tell me everything about her. She must have been an amazing woman, I mean starting a business in those days, and a prohibited one at that."

"I understand that she was indeed quite a character. She was born in Ireland at the turn of the century, and she and her husband moved here to Elm Ridge, in 1920, right about the time my grandmother was born. I'm not sure the town even had a name yet. I would have to check. Anyway, it was the spring of 1920, and everything looked good until December of that same year."

"What happened in December?"

"Her husband, my great-grandfather was one of the millions of victims of the influenza pandemic."

"Oh wow, I can't imagine what it was like with a brand-new baby and no husband in a foreign country, far away from everyone she knew!"

"She and the baby inherited the land, but she obviously couldn't farm it on her own, not while she was nursing anyway, so she went looking for a job and was hired by a man who held one of the ten government-issued licenses to produce whiskey for medicine."

"So, she did start during the prohibition, but it was legal activity?" Grace asked.

"Well, sort of," Colton said with a mischievous grin. "Next Green barbecue, you'll need to ask my mother to tell you about her namesake and how the Red Widow Bourbon was started. She tells a better story than me, so I'll just give you the highlights. The business was passed from Julia, a.k.a. the Red Widow, to her daughters, who in turned passed it on to their daughters and so on."

"This is fascinating, I'll be sure to ask your mother about it if I ever get a chance."

"Of course you will," he answered, as if her staying in Elm Ridge and being invited to another party was a done deal. "And we're almost here."

He drove away from the main road, and for a minute or so, Grace wondered where he was taking her. They were literally in the middle of nowhere, but then he drove into a clearing and the parking lot of what seemed to be a very popular place, if she was to judge by the number of cars around.

"This is the best restaurant in the state," Colton declared as he opened the car door for her. "People usually have to wait for weeks to get a table here."

"And you don't?"

"Nope, because Bailey is the *sous chef*," he declared with so much pride Grace found it cute.

"Your cousin Bailey? The one I met at your uncle's place? But she looks like she can't be a day over eighteen!"

"She does, right? But she's not. She's twenty-two, and since she began her apprenticeship very early, she's an old hand at it now."

"An old hand at twenty-two. Who knew that was even possible?"

The restaurant was set in an oddly shaped house that must have been someone's home at some point in time. Whomever came up with the concept for the place had decided to leave some of the partitions up making for smaller dining rooms and a more intimate setting. The waiter led them through a couple of those rooms to a table in a quiet corner.

Colton pulled her chair for her, and when they were settled, he said, "So, tell me more about this open book life. What's your family like?"

"The opposite of yours," she answered.

"What does that mean?"

"You said you had about fifty direct blood relatives just in the county, well I have none."

"What do you mean none? No one has no relatives!"

Grace tortured the white napkin that was beautifully folded on her plate and looked up. "Well, you're right. I did have a mother, but she's gone now, and she was an only child."

Colton caught her hand, and there was no pity but only compassion when he asked, "What about a father?"

Loving the comforting gesture, Grace held on to his hand and shook her head. "Nope. I never had the chance to meet the man who gave me half of my genetic makeup."

Grace kept to herself that her mother was unable to give her any information about him. She didn't do it out of spite or to keep some deep dark secret, but because she couldn't remember. Around the time of Grace's conception, she was either too drunk or too stoned—or maybe both—to remember whom she'd slept with.

One thing Grace would be eternally grateful to her for was her mother cleaning up her act the second she had found out she was expecting. She had stayed clean until Grace turned ten. During those years she was a born-again health nut.

"Your body is your temple," she would say while serving them homemade meals of white rice and steamed vegetables and insisting that sugar was the devil incarnate.

Despite the lack of sweets at home, which had Grace

acting like a starved lunatic at birthday parties, those were happy years. But then something happened. Grace never found out what, but whatever it was, it broke her mother's resolve, and she desecrated her temple again.

But no one ever wants to hear about stuff like that, so Grace gave him the edited version, "My mother passed away very young. Cancer."

She glided over the details of her deadly trilogy—hep C followed by cirrhosis, which in turn became liver cancer.

"I'm so sorry," he said, squeezing her hand a little harder before letting go.

The waiter returned with the menu and two flutes of champagne offered by the house and then listed the specials of the day.

After he had taken their order, Colton asked, "How did you manage to put yourself through college and then law school with no one to help you?"

"Scholarships for college," she said. "And then I met Sam."

"Sam?"

"My ex-husband."

"You were married?" Surprise and disappointment laced the question. It was subtle, but Grace could feel something in his behavior change, even as he asked, "Should we skip the subject altogether?"

"No, it's fine. The separation was amicable," Grace explained. "What can you do when your spouse falls out of love? Nothing but let him go."

"You never considered fighting to fix your marriage?" Colton protested.

"Oh, believe me, if I had thought I stood a chance I would have," she snapped back, hurt by the clear accusation.

Grace was not a quitter. She would have given it all she

had if she had thought it was the right thing to do. But it wasn't, so Grace didn't even try. As soon as he said that *the other woman* was expecting his child, she had surrendered.

"But..."

Bailey's arrival cut the conversation short.

"It's such a nice surprise to see you again," she said to Grace. "I just came for a second. I wanted to say hello before things got crazy in the kitchen."

They chitchatted for a minute, and when Bailey left there was an awkward silence.

Had they not been in the middle of nowhere, and had the chef not been her boss' daughter, Grace would have claimed a migraine and made a run for it. That was something she shared with Ashton Green. They were both ridden with horrible migraines. She did her best to never use her condition as an excuse for fear that fate would punish her by giving her a really bad one.

Talking about her failed marriage had broken the mood. Colton had withdrawn. Yes, something was broken, but she would survive. She always did.

Interesting how Colton didn't seem to care that she was a love child but was unable to deal with the fact that she'd been married. Clearly his interest in her had vanished the second he figured out she was divorced. Those things certainly didn't happen in his family!

The conversation took a more superficial turn, and she was disappointed.

She shouldn't be. What she needed to do was enjoy being placed in the friend zone.

Grace was sure he would make a wonderful friend, and friends were just what she needed.

While she ate scrumptious food and listened to him talk about Elm Ridge history, the very safe topic of conversation toward which she'd steered their conversation, Grace reminded herself that for him, family would always come first, and that they could never be anything more than buddies.

It was better this way since a family was one thing she could never offer.

CHAPTER 16

GRACE

The GPS helped Grace find the Green horse training facility, and she was reminded of her first Green barbecue. Was it only a month earlier? There was a major difference between then and now. This time, she would know many of the people present.

The first person she ran into when she left her car was Mackenzie.

"Grace!" She hugged her like a long-lost sister.

Her demonstration of affection was so spontaneous that Grace hugged her back without reservation.

"I didn't know you were in town," Grace said.

"I flew back in yesterday with the boys. I was going to drop in on you at your office as soon as I got settled in but, hey, you're here, so that's even better."

"You brought your sons with you? How nice. Gunner must be over the moon." He had been like an excited kid when he found out she named her eldest after him.

"I'll introduce you when they reappear," she said, taking Grace by the arm to walk towards the crowd. "Gunner has taken them to the stables to look at the ponies. We only have big horses at home, and he thought that their first ride should be on a smaller animal."

A few guests Grace didn't know came to greet Mackenzie as if she were visiting royalty. Mackenzie made introductions and after they were gone observed, "It's so strange to be back. I could never say that to any of them, but it feels as if they have remained frozen. I've been gone for more than ten years, and it's as if I'd left yesterday. I swear, everything seems the same."

"Funny you should say that because that's one thing I've noticed since I've arrived. Time is different here than in the big cities." Indeed, during the first couple of weeks, Grace had felt as if she was living in slow motion. Then she adapted. She started to like taking her time. Grace thought it was luxurious to not rush through everything.

But just as she was getting the hang of it, time slowed down a bit more. Why? Because Colton had vanished.

Of course, he didn't actually disappear. Grace knew that. He was simply gone on a business trip for a bit over a week, but he never said anything about it—well, not to her. Not that he should have, but still, Grace was sort of hoping to hear from him after their dinner.

"Time passes differently here," she added thoughtfully.

Mackenzie looked over her shoulder and said, "I need to go check on the kids."

Grace turned around to see what Mackenzie was looking at and spotted a pack of Green brothers coming in their direction.

Colton was among them, but he hadn't seen her yet. He was busy talking to Braxton, the very handsome veterinarian. There was something incredible about that man. He looked good enough to make the cover of GQ magazine. Yet, he wasn't the one who had caught her attention.

They both turned in opposite directions. Grace didn't

know who Mackenzie was running away from, but she seemed to be in as much of a hurry as Grace herself was.

For some reason Grace thought that Colton was not due back before Monday. She had misunderstood. How could she have thought he wouldn't be around? Sunday barbecues were like religious celebrations for the Green clan. The sole member absent was Weston, and that was only because he had an extenuating circumstance: he was serving his country in some foreign and hostile land.

Since their dinner or date, whatever it had been, Grace had given Colton a lot of thought. Her attraction to him puzzled her to no end. She'd never been one to fall head over heels for anyone. Even as a teenager, she'd never believed in insta-love like most of her friends did. As an adult, she thought love at first sight was something made up by Hollywood scriptwriters. Now, she was starting to wonder.

There was no denying that the simple thought of him made her giddy, while—if she attempted to be objective—she didn't know much about the man. Not much at all. So, it didn't make sense for her to feel this way. And yet she did.

Maybe she was better off sticking with Mackenzie. Retracing her steps, she was delighted to bump into Willow's friendly face. "Can you show me where the stables are? Mackenzie is there with her kids and her brother."

"That's the twins you reconciled, right?"

"You know I can't talk about that," Grace chided her new friend.

"But you don't need to." Willow's voice was all good humor. "I know all about what you did."

"You do?"

"Oh, yeah. It's been the talk of the town for the entire week," Willow explained. "Friday, at the Gumbo La Ya, Sandy was telling everyone who would listen that you had cast a spell on them."

Grace laughed. "And what did Gloria say?"

"That you had worked your magic, but that it was not witchcraft, just pure talent."

It was such a sweet compliment, Grace blushed.

"Now, don't let it go to your head," Willow mocked and patted her in the shoulder.

"I promise, I won't."

There was no miracle-working on her part. The love between those two was so strong that they would have reunited with or without her. She had just acted as a catalyst and made it happen faster.

"Now, you have some explaining to do, young lady," she said. "Where were you on Friday night? You know you're not allowed to skip our girls' night out without a very good excuse."

Grace didn't have one. She'd stayed home alone, and that had been stupid of her. There was nothing to mope about, as her priority was to get her life in order and learn to enjoy being single again.

That's right, she was not moping. She simply needed some alone time.

Time to think about Colton.

Colton who had shown some interested in her, or so she had thought, and then lost it.

Right, but even if he was interested, she was not.

She didn't want a relationship.

Maybe if she repeated that often enough, she'd manage to convince herself.

CHAPTER 17

COLTON

What was with this woman?

When she first rushed away as he arrived, Colton thought she hadn't seen him, but for the split second when they'd made eye contact, there was no mistaking her attitude. She was avoiding him. Why else would she dash in the opposite direction only a few seconds after his arrival? He would never understand women.

"Do you have any idea where Willow and Grace went?" Colton asked Audrey .

"Nope, but if you see Willow let her know I'm heading to the kitchen in case they need some help."

"Will do."

Colton turned around and ran into Jaxon listening to one of the guests rambling about their son's science fair project and how excited he was to attend camp here soon.

Noticing his brother's *save me* look, he interrupted the woman just as her mouth opened to prattle about on about who knew what. "Excuse me, ma'am," he said, resting his hand on his brother's arm, "but Jaxon's needed in the stables."

"Anything wrong?" the woman asked.

"Nope, not a thing. It's just that Jaxon has to interview a new stable boy," Colton reassured her.

Jaxon looked at his watch as if checking the time and apologized, "I'm so sorry. I totally forgot about that."

They both turned in direction of the stables. Jaxon winked at him and whispered, "I owe you one."

"I'm looking for Grace," Colton told his brother.

"Then we're going in the right direction. I saw her and Willow on their way to the stables just a few minutes ago."

Jaxon accompanied him until they reached a small corral where Gunner was helping a young boy climb on a pony. Willow and Grace were standing at the perimeter as well as—

"Mackenzie?" Colton called out.

She turned around and ran in their direction. "Colton, Jaxon, my goodness, it's so good to see you again."

A little boy ran by her side, and Colton travelled back in time. He had no doubt whose son he was. Mackenzie had produced a miniature replica of her twin. Colton looked at the other young boy in the corral. He also looked like a Cox.

"Your boys?" he asked.

"Yep," she answered proudly.

She turned around and called the little boy who had remained a few step backs.

"Jack, come and say hello to my friends," she called out.

"You look just like your uncle, you know," Colton told him.

He glanced towards the corral and shook his head as if to indicate that grownups were so silly sometimes.

"Not now, of course, but when he was your age," Colton explained.

"Ah!" That seems to make more sense. He frowned and asked, "Then did Mama get our name wrong?"

"What do you mean?"

"If I look like him," he pointed with his chin towards his uncle, "then I should be Gunner and Gunner should be Jack, no?"

It took Colton a second to catch on, but he finally did. Mackenzie had named her eldest after her brother.

"Maybe not," he answered. "That could have been too confusing since you look like him so much."

Mackenzie laughed, and he asked her, "How old are they?"

"Gunner's eight, and I'm six," Jack answered.

"Do you want to ride too?" Jaxon asks him.

"Of course, I do, but I can't right now."

"Why not?"

"Because Uncle Gunner said I had to wait for my turn," he explained with the tone children take to speak to adults when they're not sure how smart they are.

"But what if I accompanied you to pick your own horse?"

"You can do that?"

"Yes, I can. I own this place," Jaxon answered.

"Mama, can we?" he asked.

"Yes, my love, we can," Mackenzie answered, following him and Jaxon in the direction of the stables.

"Willow," Colton called out taking a few steps toward her and Grace. "Audrey asks to let you know she'll be in the kitchen."

Willow jumped down from the corral fence and leaned into Grace. "She must want to talk about something. I'd better go see what kind of crazy is happening now."

Grace was about to follow her when Colton stopped her.

"Hey there, why are you avoiding me?"

She tilted her head and frowned.

"Did I do something to upset you?"

Colton could almost hear the wheels turning in her head as she decided how to answer. That was bad news.

"No really, you didn't," she said.

Obviously, it was worse than he thought.

"Except...," he prompted.

That trick usually worked with Sophia, but Grace saw right through it and laughed.

"Okay," she admitted. "I'm not mad. I was simply disappointed not to hear back from you after our da—dinner."

And now their evening together had been downgraded from a date to a dinner. Damage control was required.

"I'm sorry. I left the next day, and then time sort of flew by and..."

She raised her hand and cut him short. "It's fine, really, don't worry. Did you have a nice trip?"

"Very productive and—"

"Colton," Jaxon called out as he returned with Mackenzie and Jack sitting bareback on his oldest mare.

He held the bridle in one hand and rested his other hand for reassurance on the young boy's leg.

"Can you open the corral door for our new rider, please?"

"Sure thing!"

Taking a step toward him, Colton stopped and turned around. "Are you going to vanish again?" he asked Grace.

"Probably," she answered. "But the party just started. I'm sure we'll run into each other a few times."

"Fair enough. I'll find you later then."

And they would have to have a talk about expectations and how to voice them to avoid disappointment.

CHAPTER 18

GRACE

The phone chimed just as Grace opened her front door.

A text from Colton.

You vanished again :-(

She laughed. She hadn't. Well, not immediately. She stayed around long enough to grab a quick bite to eat and snatch a piece of Sophia's chocolate cake to take home for breakfast.

What about lunch tomorrow?

Sorry, no. I'll be in court all day.

Grace slammed the door behind her and put the cake on the table next to the files she had brought home from the office—an exception to her rule. She needed to study them again to be ready for the following day.

The phone beeped again.

Then dinner Friday night?

I have a thing already Friday night.

I know. Willow's surprise birthday party @ the Gumbo La Ya. I'm invited too. We can go together.

Actually, that sounded good. She would be able to have a drink without wondering about the drive back.

Sounds like a plan.

Grace put the phone down and got comfy to give a last review of her case. She was ready. She knew she was, but she wanted to be absolutely certain.

The phone rang. It took a few seconds for her brain to engage after identifying the tone. The Elvis ringtone meant a call from Sam. After the divorce, she had changed his ring tone from *Love Me Tender* to *Trouble*.

What did he want from her? Only one way to find out. She stood to ready herself for a possible confrontation.

"Hello." She kept her voice as neutral as she could.

"Hey, Honey Bunch, how are you doing?"

Well, actually pretty well. His voice no longer made her weak in the knees. Also, his use of terms of endearment to address her simply annoyed her whereas it used to exasperate her. She mentally patted herself on the back. This was progress.

"Fine." She toyed with the idea of asking how he was but decided to dispense with the small talk and get straight to the point. "To what do I owe the honor of your call?"

"Oh!"

Part of her was happy to have surprised him with her abrupt answer, but it didn't last long. Sam was like a cat. No matter what the situation, he always ended up on his feet.

"It's about our place."

Yep. She'd figured that was the case since it was the only thing they had in common these days. He'd gotten to keep all the rest—the friends, the furniture, and even the photo albums. Grace hadn't wanted anything that would have reminded her of him.

"What about our place?"

"Well..."

His pause made her heart beat faster, and not in a pleasant way. Darn, she knew she had forgotten something. She had wanted to check the mortgage payment. Every so often, she would blame herself for making a very bad decision about that place.

Shortly after the separation, he had offered to pay for the mortgage, the maintenance, and the real estate taxes if she were to allow him to keep living there. Of course, she had agreed, but not out of the goodness of her heart. Well, a little but not solely. She agreed mainly because it seemed like a decent offer at the time. The rent for a place like theirs did run a little under what he'd offered to pay. Also, she had figured real estate in Manhattan was a rather safe investment.

She had been an idiot. She never thought about the damage he could do to her credit rating if he started missing the payments. She never imagined he would miss any. He was the one who came from money, not her!

"I found a buyer for our place."

"A buyer?" She counted to three in her head to keep her cool. "I don't remember us deciding to put it on the market. You didn't list it without asking me first, did you?"

"Absolutely not!"

"So?"

"So what?"

"How did you find a buyer?" Grace rolled her eyes at his short attention span.

"Oh, that. I didn't actually find him," Sam explained. "He found me. There's this new guy who has been buying several apartments in the building, two on our floor, and—"

It sounded like a long story, one so long she didn't have the patience for it.

"How much is he offering?" she cut in.

"Well, that's what I want to talk to you about," Sam answered with the very condescending tone he liked to use when he wanted to assert his superiority.

Grace swallowed an exasperated sigh and bit back the few nasty retorts that had come immediately to mind. Instead, she just said, "I'm listening."

"The offer is good. It's better than good, it's amazing!"

And here came the sales pitch.

"But there's one hitch—"

Of course, Sam's amazing deals always came with a couple of those. That's how he had lost most of the money he'd inherited from his grandmother. Maybe it was all of that money by now.

"—he wants all the paperwork done in a weeks' time."

"Why the rush?" Her very legitimate question fell on a deaf ear.

"That's a week from tomorrow."

"Yes, Sam, I understand what one week means."

"Would you be okay to sell, Gracie?" he cooed. "It's such a great opportunity. I don't want to let it pass. Please?"

Just a year ago Grace would have said yes without giving it a second thought. Hell, Grace would have said yes just to make him happy. Today, she didn't care about his happiness anymore, and she wanted to take time to consider her options.

"I'm not sure."

"Gracie," he pleaded.

"Why don't you send me the offer, and I'll have a look at it."

"Don't you get all lawyerly on me now, Ms. Baker," he growled.

She laughed into the phone without trying to hide it.

"Send me the offer. Or better yet, if they want the deal done by next Monday, have them send me a draft of the contract."

No use telling him that it was unlikely they would close on Monday. Monday was July third. Most people would be taking a five-day weekend. For her, it would be a mini vacation since Green and Partners would remain closed on that day.

"Okayyyy…" He drew out the last syllable to make it sound as if she was being difficult.

She didn't think she was.

No. She didn't *think*, she was sure she was being very reasonable.

And that very thought made her feel liberated. She had an epiphany; she was cured. She no longer cared about what he thought. She would do what was best for her.

"I'll email you back after I've reviewed the paperwork," she said. "You have a nice evening."

She hung up and screamed with joy. She didn't even care if Mrs. Carson heard her. In a few weeks, she would no longer have to deal with her grumpy landlord. And if the offer Sam received was legit, she would accept it and sever the last knot that tied her to New York and her previous life, and maybe, well, maybe she could think of growing roots in this new town.

CHAPTER 19

COLTON

Once again, Colton parked in front of the Carson house, but this time he ignored the movement of the curtains when Mrs. Carson checked to see who was walking up her driveway.

Nevertheless, the old lady opened her door and took a couple of steps out.

"She's not home yet," she announced.

"Good afternoon, Mrs. Carson. How are you today?"

"Didn't you hear me? I said she's not home."

"That's fine," he answered. "I'll wait."

She was about to say something but was interrupted by the arrival of Grace's miniature car.

She parked on the street and rushed towards them. With her navy suit and her hair up in a bun, she looked like a formidable businesswoman.

"Good evening, Mrs. Carson," she said.

"I told you I didn't want to be disturbed," her landlady snapped. "That meant no visitors."

"Absolutely," Grace answered with a large smile. "I have not forgotten the terms of my lease, and I can assure you that Colton's not visiting. He's just picking me up."

"Semantics," Mrs. Carson growled with a disgusted tone that made Colton want to laugh.

"We'll be gone in a minute," Grace insisted before turning to him. "I'm so sorry I lost track of time at the office. Would you give me a minute to change into something more comfortable?"

"Absolutely. Why don't I wait for you in my car?"

Grace turned towards the old witch and said, "See, not visiting."

Mrs. Carson retreated into her home and slammed the door behind her. Grace winked at Colton and hurried to her side of the house, leaving him alone in the driveway.

Grace could take care of herself. He loved the way she held her ground while remaining pleasant. Walking back to his car to wait for her, Colton realized that he had actually enjoyed watching her defend herself.

He leaned against his truck and waited. She rushed out a few minutes later in a green summer dress that matched perfectly the color of her eyes. Her hair flowing freely around her shoulders made her look younger and carefree.

"That was fast," Colton opening the door for her.

"A little more than the promised minute, but we'll still be there before Willow," she said. "Sophia says she's found a few excuses to make sure they would arrive later than the rest of the group."

"Oh, I'm sure she has. My sister is very resourceful when she needs to be."

He closed the door and walked around the car wondering when would be the best time for the little talk he thought they should have. By the time he started the car, he had decided that it was better to do it right away to clear the air.

"So, last Sunday," he started.

Grace sat up a little straighter but didn't say anything.

"You did do your best to avoid me," Colton stated with a tone that was affirmative enough for her to understand there would be no point in denying it. "And I've been wondering all week what the heck it was that I had done to upset you."

With a quick glance in her direction, Colton saw the tension in her shoulders lessen, but she still didn't say anything.

"I really like you, Grace, and the last thing I wanted to do was to offend you, so if I have, would you mind telling me how, so I don't do it again?"

She sighed and looked through her side window.

"Come on," he pleaded.

She took a big breath and turned her face towards him to answer. "You didn't do anything wrong." She raised her hand in a gesture he understood to indicate she was not done but was just searching for her words. "No, you didn't, really. What happened is your entire attitude changed when I told you I had been married."

Colton thought back to their first date conversation and realized she might have a point.

"The way you reacted when I told you I thought my only course of action was to let my husband go... You made it sound as if I was a quitter, and I was—hurt is too big a word —upset is probably more appropriate."

Colton let a few seconds pass before answering.

"You're right," he recognized. "My behavior was probably different after you told me you were divorced, but that's because it got me thinking. I was wondering how fresh your wounds were and if it wasn't too early for you to start dating again."

"Oh."

With his eyes on the road, Colton couldn't catch her

expression, but she sounded surprised. Surprised in a pleasant way, like she hadn't considered that possibility.

"I know I'm repeating myself, but I like you very much, and what I needed to find out, what I still need to find out, is if you've turned the page or if I should slow down and wait a bit before letting you know about my intentions."

"That is sweet and considerate," she said slowly.

"Well, I am a sweet and considerate man," he panned back with a humorous tone.

She laughed at his tooting his own horn and looked away, out through the side window again.

"So, what is it Grace? Are you still mourning your marriage?"

She shook her head.

"Nah, that ship has sailed. It's done and over with, or at least it will be as soon as we sell our apartment."

"Did you put it up for sale?"

"It's complicated," she said. "Selling it wasn't in the plan initially, but you know what they say, life happens while we're busy making plans."

They reached the restaurant, and while he looked for a parking spot Grace said, "I did not come here to get away from Sam. He's no longer a factor in my decisions. I came here to build a new life." She remained silent for a bit before declaring with conviction. "Yes, I want a new life for myself."

Good. That was perfect. She did say she wanted a new life for herself and not a life on her own.

With a little help, she could find a place for a new man in that new life of hers.

CHAPTER 20

GRACE

He opened the door for her and offered his hand for her to get out. Grace hesitated but took it. It was just a hand and a friendly gesture. Except that when he held on to her hand, she no longer felt innocent. She looked up to him and saw a hunger there that probably matched her own.

Her mental waver made her unstable, and he caught her.

"What's the matter, Grace?" he whispered, holding her so close she couldn't breathe.

She shook her head.

"Uh-uh," he said. "You need to learn to communicate better."

That got a laugh out of her.

Seriously? She was a master communicator. If she hadn't spent years perfecting that skill, she would never had become certified as a mediator.

Colton seemed to understand her reaction and frowned.

"I'm not talking about Counselor Grace. That woman is incredible. How she managed to convince Mackenzie not to ask for anything more than the shack on the lake, I guess I'll never know."

Grace opened her mouth to protest that she didn't have to talk her into anything, but she closed it without uttering a syllable. No matter how much she wanted to explain that she had been nothing more than a catalyst, that it was never Mackenzie's intention to claim the half of the property she was rightfully entitled to, she couldn't say a thing. Rules of ethics prevented her from sharing anything she had learned while acting as their mediator.

"I'm talking about Ms. Grace Baker." Colton stopped and asked, "Is Baker your maiden name?"

She nodded. Even when she had been married, she had remained Grace Baker. Strangely, she had never felt the need to change her name. In hindsight, she wondered if that meant she hadn't been committed enough to the marriage. Unless it meant she unconsciously knew it wouldn't last. Who knew?

"Good, so Ms. Baker, the very private Ms. Baker, should try to open up a bit more."

Grace pushed her head back a little to get a better look at him. He was still holding her in his arms. Anyone looking at them would have believed they had decided to start dancing in the parking lot.

"What do you want to know?" Grace asked.

"Everything," he said.

"That's a tall order."

"It doesn't have to be filled tonight, Grace." He caressed her cheek tenderly. "We have an entire life ahead of us."

Her breath caught in her throat, and she was at a loss for words.

"For tonight, I'll be satisfied to learn about your short-term expectations," he added, lowering his head towards hers. He acted so smoothly that she felt as if time had stopped. Life took on a slow-motion quality. Wild thoughts raced around her head. Deep down, she knew falling for a man like him was wrong—very wrong—but for the life of her, she couldn't remember why.

Right that instant, the only thing she knew was she wanted to feel his lips on hers, wanted him to hold her tighter, wanted *him*. And so, even though she had all the time in the world to do so, she didn't turn her head away, and when his lips gently landed on hers, she shivered in the spring evening. Her hands fisted in his shirt as she leaned into him and breathed him in. Time stopped. But just for a moment.

Colton pulled away, and the clock started ticking again.

"Shall we go in?" he asked gently.

She nodded, too shaken to trust her voice with a coherent answer.

The following hours were a merry blur. Most of the Gumbo La Ya had been commandeered by the Green family and the staff of the Green horse training facility. The Cox twins were there too, and Mackenzie was quite the party girl dancing with all the Green brothers one by one.

When it was Jaxon's turn to swirl with her around the dance floor, Grace couldn't help but notice Willow watching from the sidelines, her bright smile slowly slipping away. Another moment passed and nibbling on her lower lip, Willow spin around and escaped to the ladies' room.

"Hey, birthday girl," Grace said, walking in the facilities right behind her.

"Hey, you," she answered with a forced smile.

"What's the matter?"

Willow shook her head with conviction, but Grace didn't buy her answer. She pushed open the doors of the three stalls to check that no one else was around and tried again. "It's just you and me. Spill it, girl."

"Can you let it go, please?"

"I'm not sure," Grace answered. "It's your birthday. You seemed to be happy and having fun until something clearly upset you."

"I'm fine," Willow said. "I'm just tired. It's been a tough week."

"Oh no, what happened?"

"I'm the worst dancer ever," she declared with a tone so sinister Grace had to roll her lips not to laugh.

Willow made it sound like it was the end of the world.

Before Grace had a chance to come up with a comforting answer, the door burst open revealing Sophia. "This is where you were hiding," she said, oblivious to her bestie's shining eyes. "We've been looking everywhere for you. It's time to blow out your candles."

"Give me a minute?" Willow asked, rushing into a stall.

"Okay, I'll tell the kitchen to hold on for another minute, but hurry!"

Sophia left, and Willow came out a few seconds later wiping her eyes with toilet paper.

"It's your day. Let yourself put away all the discouraging things and enjoy the celebration." Grace tried the only thing she could think of to reassure her.

"Yeah, I know you're right," Willow answered, pulling herself back together.

"Plus, don't forget, since it's your birthday, so you do get one wish!"

That brought a real smile to her face. Willow believed in good vibes and karma, so for her, wishes were serious business.

"Yes, you're right," she said, giving Grace a warm hug. "If I wish it with all my heart, I can turn my dreams into a reality."

"There you go!"

Grace opened the door for her and envied her for a second. She knew for a fact that no matter how hard you tried and how much you wanted to believe, some things were not meant to be.

CHAPTER 21

COLTON

About one in the morning, most people had decided to call it a night. Colton didn't need to look for Grace. He knew precisely where she was after keeping his eyes on her all night. He did so even when he kept his distance so as not to scare her away.

They had danced a few times, which gave him a chance to hold her tight again, but he made sure to keep the conversation light.

Grace also danced with Gunner for a while, and looking at the carefree way she behaved with him, Colton had felt a pang of jealousy. It was silly, really. He knew that even if his friend had yet to do something about it, Gunner's heart was already taken. Also, Colton had no doubt that Grace was not the sort of woman who would kiss one man on her way to a party and then attempt to seduce another a couple of hours later. Yet when Gunner made her laugh and she tilted her head back, Colton had regrets. He would have loved to be the one on the receiving end of that smile.

Grace turned to him after giving a last hug to Willow.

"All ready," she said.

"Then we'll be on our way." He waved his goodbyes to the few remaining members of the group.

As soon as they stepped out, Grace shivered and slipped her arms into her sweater. The spring night was pleasant but a bit chilly compared to the steamy atmosphere of the Gumbo La Ya. Colton took advantage of the opportunity to run his hands over her arms in a warming gesture. She looked up at him, and he was unsure about what he was reading in her lovely green eyes. He thought it was longing. Or maybe he simply hoped it was.

And it was. She let out a small sigh of disappointment when he let her go to open the car door. She wanted him to kiss her again, but not here. The parking lot was too crowded.

"Hurry in," Colton told her. "I'll put on the heat, and you'll feel better in no time."

He drove in silence for a few minutes, and when her shivers were gone, he returned to their previous conversation.

"So, can we talk about your short-term expectations?"

She turned her head towards him.

"Sleeping in," she said. "And not just tomorrow. I intend to do it for four days in a row since your uncle was sweet enough to decide he would close the office on Monday."

This would be Addison's handy work. When the July 4th family barbecue was at her place, she made sure he stayed home so that she could *delegate* most of the work to him.

"Did you make plans for this long weekend?"

"Aside from sleeping, nope." Correcting herself, she added, "Well, Mr. Green did invite the entire firm to his Fourth of July party, so I guess I do have plans for that day."

"Perfect," Colton said. "That gives you plenty of time to visit our most fascinating local attractions."

She gave him a surprised look, one that said she didn't think there was such a thing as a fascinating local attraction in

Elm Ridge. Colton couldn't blame her. His little town had done nothing to become visible on a map, and truth be told, they were all happy about that.

"I was thinking tomorrow I would take you to lunch and an exclusive private tour of the Red Widow Bourbon distillery."

"That sounds lovely."

"And then Sunday, I would like you to accompany me for a Sunday dinner at the Green ranch."

She stiffened. Maybe the family dinner was too much.

"It will be a small gathering since we're all meeting again on Tuesday. You know, at Uncle Ashton's place."

But then again, given the comparative sizes of their families, his idea of a small gathering was likely to be quite different.

Okay, Colton thought. He was going too fast. He backpedaled before she had a chance to say no.

"You know what, let's do it one day at a time," he suggested.

The look of relief on her face was such that he understood he needed to cool his horses.

He parked in front of Mrs. Carson's house and killed the engine but left the lights on while walking around the car to help her out.

"Let me walk you to your door," he said, taking her hand.

He didn't let it go as they walked up the driveway.

There was a light in one of the first-floor bedrooms.

Grace noticed and joked about it.

"I think she was waiting up for me."

From what Colton had seen of Mrs. Carson, he wouldn't put it past her to stay up all night to make sure Grace didn't bring anyone home.

"Someone has to make sure you remember there are no

visitors allowed," he chimed in as they turned the corner and reached her door.

"See, he's not visiting, he's just dropping me off," she said, addressing an imaginary Mrs. Carson.

"Right, just making sure you get home safe."

Grace smiled and picked up the rock where she kept her key. She pulled out the key chain, put the rock back in its place, and fumbled with the lock.

Mrs. Carson should have known better, Colton thought. She needed to install a small outside lamp or light above the door. He gently took the keys from Grace and managed to open the door.

"Thank you," Grace said as he placed the keys back in her hand.

"And now, I'm making sure you get a good night kiss," Colton then whispered pulling her closer to him.

She came willingly, her breath short and her lips slightly parted. Her large eyes closed as he took possession of her lips.

The first kiss had not been enough; it had done nothing more than whet his appetite. All evening he had been starving for another, and now that he had it, he was feeling an incredible hunger.

All his will power was required to put an end to their embrace, but when he did, he was rewarded with the softest smile she'd given him yet—a smile that held a thousand promises. She placed her two hands lightly on his chest and gently pushed him away.

"No visitors," she said.

Right, and now that he thought about it, he was grateful for Mrs. Carson's presence and her acting as a proverbial watchdog.

A woman like Grace was too precious not to be protected.

CHAPTER 22

GRACE

It was eleven when Grace's phone chirped. *Colton.*

Can you be ready for noon?

She stretched and thought about it. There were a few things she needed to do, the first being to read the notes on the contract draft Sam had sent earlier in the week. She had asked one of her New York friends who knew about real estate law to check on it and hadn't had a chance to look at it yet.

Would one be okay?

Absolutely. See you then.

Grace sighed and stretched, again savoring the warmth of her bed while reflecting on yesterday.

Part of her felt like dancing and screaming with joy because now she knew for sure that she was totally, absolutely, definitively over Sam. That very same part felt giddy like a silly teenager.

Colton liked her.

Colton liked her, and he wanted to get to know her better.

Colton liked her, and...

That's where the other part of her kicked in.

If there was one thing she had come to understand since she'd moved to Elm Ridge, it was that people were different.

In New York, people like her raced for everything.

She had raced to get picked by one of the top law firms because only *if* she made the cut would she get a chance to make enough to repay her student loans before she reached retirement age.

But she had only been able to enter that race because she'd first won the law school race. And to win that first race, she had needed to come out of the right college, which was harder to attend without first going to the right high school, which one could only be admitted to if one lived in the right part of town or had affluent enough parents.

Those who didn't, well, they were out of luck unless they had a very specific talent—one that allowed them to run twice as fast.

Here, it looked like everyone was taking life at a more leisurely pace. Of course, everyone worked. No doubt about it. Most worked really hard too. The difference was that here everyone was expected to have a life outside of work.

She and Ashton Green had talked about it when she visited for her first interview. He had explained that he didn't care if the lawyers he hired had graduated from one of the top ten law schools in the country or what their GPA had been in college. He cared about who those people were.

"Those people I'm hiring," he said, "they will move to Elm Ridge and settle here. They will make friends, fall in love, have children, and maybe leave my firm to start their own business. One way or another, they will become part of this community, and what this community needs is not necessarily a bunch of competitive hyper-achievers. Nah, what we need are team players, good people we all can rely on."

Grace thought he didn't say it outright because he was

afraid of scaring her or sounding too corny, but what he meant was that he considered the people he hired as members of his family, and that, in the end, family was all that mattered.

Family… Right… Grace needed to put the final nail in the proverbial coffin of the family she had attempted to build with Sam. She switched on her old laptop she'd brought back from the office the day before. While the antique machine booted, she jumped in the shower.

When she was done, she opened the initial version of the contract Sam had sent and then the annotated version returned by her friend to go through her comments and approve of the changes she proposed. When she had an acceptable finalized version, one she would be willing to sign, she emailed it back to Sam.

Rats! It was five to one, and she was still wrapped up in her towel. There was barely time to brush her hair, jump into a pair of jeans and a tee shirt, and put on her boots before there was a knock on the door.

She opened the door, ready to look up into Colton's smiling face, but no. She had to look down on Mrs. Carson's frowning mug. Determined not to let anyone spoil her positive mood, Grace greeted her with a cheery tone.

"Good morning, Mrs. Carson, how are you today?"

"Very unhappy," the old witch snapped back.

"I'm sorry to hear that," Grace answered with all the compassion she could muster, which sadly wasn't much.

Mrs. Carson tilted her head, waiting for Grace to ask her what seemed to be the trouble, but she didn't oblige. If the old lady was set on making her life difficult, she was not about to make it easier for her. They stared at each other in silence until Mrs. Carson caved in.

"I told you I didn't want visitors," she stated, enunciating each syllable as if she wasn't sure Grace understood English properly.

Grace remained silent, and that seemed to infuriate her landlord even more.

"It's in your lease, and I reminded you last night when I caught you on your way out."

Gritting her teeth to keep from barking back at her, Grace slowly counted to ten in her head.

"But you didn't listen, and then you had to bring the Green mongrel back home with you in the middle of the night."

Now, it didn't happen often, but she was just about to lose her cool. There were very few things that would make her fly off the handle, and the use of the word *bastard* was one of them. Bastard, mongrel, spurious, or even baseborn—it was all the same to her, and she could not tolerate it.

"Let's make this very clear now, Mrs. Carson," Grace said with her coldest voice. She leaned forward and looked menacing enough to force Mrs. Carson to take a defensive step back.

"First, I have been an exemplary tenant. Second, I have not had any visitors *ever* in my studio. Third, the only person who has come here to pick me up and walk me back to my door to make sure I got home safely was a gentleman, and I will not let you insult him."

Mrs. Carson opened her mouth to answer, but something caught her attention. Colton had just turned the corner of the building.

The old lady mumbled something barely understandable about sleeping with dogs and picking up fleas and walked away in the opposite direction.

"What in tarnation was that all about?" he asked.

"You walking me back to my door last night," Grace answered, watching Mrs. Carson rush away.

She turned toward Colton, who looked scrumptious in a nicely cut pair of black jeans and a pale blue denim shirt. For a second, she forgot what she had set out to do, and then it came back to her—bag, sweater, *go girl go*.

"Give me a second to pick up my bag, and I'll be ready to go."

When she returned a few seconds later, he was leaning against the door frame with an amused grin on his face.

He took the key from her hands, locked the door, placed the set in its usual hiding place, and chuckled as he asked, "So I'm a gentleman, hey?"

CHAPTER 23

COLTON

"Well, I thought you were," Grace answered playfully. "But now that I realize you eavesdrop on conversations, I may have to revise my judgment."

Colton took on a mock contrite expression and placed his hand on the small of her back to lead her toward his truck.

"But I do love the way you've flipped the table on us," Colton said.

"What do you mean?" she asked.

"That I love the way you turned yourself into my lady in shining armor when you thought I was a knight in distress."

She laughed and executed a perfect bow.

"Milady, your chariot awaits," he said, taking her hand to help her hop in.

She gave his hand a little squeeze and answered, "Thank you, milord."

After closing the car door behind her, Colton turned around to look back on the wicked witch's castle and, true to form, Mrs. Carson was standing by her door, arms akimbo, glaring at them.

He shook his head, and for a second wondered why she

was being so nasty. There might be some past history he didn't know about, possibly something between her and his mother. He could ask. He could, but he wouldn't. She was not worth losing time over.

"So," he said, joining Grace in the car, "we shall start with a brief but very instructive tour of the Red Widow facilities, and then we'll have lunch."

"This sounds perfect."

"The first thing you need to know is that it all starts with the water. You see, part of the state is on a limestone bed, and the water filters through it. When the water passes through the limestone, it removes the iron and adds calcium, which is great 'cause iron would make the Bourbon bitter while calcium gives it a sweet flavor."

She nodded with an amused smile, and suddenly Colton wondered if he was not a horrible pontificating bore.

"But maybe you don't want to know all of that."

"Of course, I do," she protested. "If I'm going to grow new roots in Kentucky, I need to know what sort of soil I'm digging in."

"You're sure?"

"Oh, absolutely!"

So, on the way to the distillery he told her about the Baxter, Crider, and Maury soil and explained what was the best for growing grains, tobacco, and corn, and which one made for the best pasture land.

The frown on her brow made him realize he was probably going into too much, detail but since they had arrived at his place, he dropped the geology topic to point to the various buildings.

"They started out with this smaller stone construction," he said pointing to the two-floor structure that was now his home. "And as the business grew, they built this red brick monstrosity."

"It does have a lot of personality," she observed.

"That it does," he agreed. "The various shades of red tell of the age of each part of the building and how anarchy presided over each extension." He sighed and pointed to a vacant spot. "In a perfect world, I would like to build a modern facility over there. Then, I would tear up this eyesore and build my dream house."

"What would your dream house be like?" she asked.

"Open, full of light, almost like a greenhouse."

She nodded enthusiastically as if she too had dreamed all her life of living in a glass house.

While she looked around at the scenery—which was magnificent as long as you had your back to the ancient structure—he opened the main door for them.

"Of course, my dream home is absolutely huge because, you know, this family does take the whole *be fruitful and multiply*' thing very seriously," he added lightly, entering the building.

Grace followed him, squinting as she adjusted from the mid-day glare to the relative indoor obscurity.

"Some facilities are open on Sundays for tourists who follow the Bourbon trail, and others operate twenty-four hours a day, seven days a week to keep up with the demand, but that's not us."

"Would you want it to be you?" she asked.

"To open for the Bourbon trail? Why not? If we're asked, we'll sure consider it. For now, we only organize visits for our local schools and of course very private guests," he answered, winking at her.

She smiled, but he could tell something was wrong.

"Is everything okay?"

"Sure," she answered, turning her back to him to look around the room. "And what about growing your business to a twenty-four hour a day, seven days a week operation? Is that what you're aiming for?"

That was a tough question, one that had kept the entire family debating late at night on many occasions.

"Some of us do," Colton explained. "Weston and I agree that we need to bring the business into the 21st century, while my mother would be happy to keep things the way they are."

"Does she say why?" Grace asked, turning around to look at him again.

"Nah, it's just a *'Let's not fix something that's not broken'* mentality," he answered, making quotes with his fingers.

"And did you explain to her why you want to grow?"

"That we did." Colton laughed. "We have hundreds of reasons to do so, but the only one which could sway her a bit is the fact that Carson and Hudson could be tempted to move to the city to find a job if the business doesn't develop enough to have an interesting position to offer them."

"That doesn't surprise me. It's clear that, for the Green clan, family is everything."

Her tone was a little sad. Did she wonder what she missed out on being raised by a single mother with no relatives whatsoever? Colton couldn't even begin to imagine how lonely that must have been, especially during the holidays. Of course, when he was a teenager, he had often felt crowded, but the truth was, he loved every single member of the tribe, even the most exasperating cousins.

"Let's get back to Bourbon," she said, pointing towards the back of the plant. "Where does it start?"

"After the water, it starts with the corn." He pointed at one of the large tanks. "The first thing is to check the corn. Bourbon is at least 51% corn. You want to make sure there's no mold or weird bacteria. So, we sort and clean the corn, and once that's done, we crush it into a meal. The idea is to break the kernel to get to the starch."

"What is that?" she asked, pointing to the mash tub.

"This is where we mix the ground corn with our magical Kentucky water. We boil the water and then add the corn, the rye, and the barley, and that's how we make our mash."

"It looks like a giant pressure cooker," she observed.

"That's precisely what it is."

"What happens after you cook everything?"

"Well, first we let it cool down, and then we add the yeast."

"Like a yogurt?"

"Exactly, and the strain of yeast is fundamental. It's always the same strain. Every time you make a new batch, you inoculate it with the old batch."

"Right, bakers do that too."

"Did you work in a bakery?" Colton asked.

"No, never, but my mother went through a do-your-own-bread phase after her do-your-own-yogurt one. She taught me all there was to learn about yeast and baking at that time," she said. "To start her own batch of yeast, she had us drive to upstate New York and walk the container in the woods for hours. She thought the bacteria it would pick up there would be better than the city ones."

Gosh, her mom sounded like she was an original, but then again, she was probably right. As long as you're going to trust the environment to ferment your food, you might as well go to a place where the air is somehow pure.

"It sounds like she was quite a character."

Grace shrugged and didn't comment further, which he took as a hint the subject was closed and he should continue his presentation.

"The yeast is going to consume the sugar liberated during the mashing process. This is going to produce heat, CO_2, and, of course, alcohol." They moved slowly along the equipment. "After three to five days, when all the sugar has been eaten up by the yeast, we have distiller's beer, and that's where the distillation process starts."

"How does this work?"

Since she seemed genuinely interested, he showed her where they fed the distiller beer before it was heated up twice to obtain the low wine and then the high wine.

They retraced their steps toward the door, and Colton heard the engine of a car arriving. Lunch was ready.

"And before I show you what happens next, I have a surprise for you," he said, leading her back into the sunlight.

CHAPTER 24

GRACE

The high sun blinded at Grace for a minute, and then she saw a minivan sporting the colors of a delivery service. A man was pulling out two trays from the back of the van and looking expectantly at Colton who pointed him further down the colossal building.

"You're right on time," he complimented the delivery man while sliding a large door open.

Right behind the door, there were two tables covered with white linen cloth. One was empty and the other one was set for two with very pretty plates and what seemed to be crystal glasses. The largest table was positioned close enough to the door to have some light while remaining in the shade, the other a bit further away.

The man delicately put the boxes on the empty table, took a tip from Colton, and vanished, wishing them a *bon appétit.*

"Shall we?" Colton asked, pulling out a chair for her.

"Of course," Grace answered, taking her seat. "I'm very impressed."

"I'm glad," he answered with a wink. "You see, I can set a

table, make reservations, and possibly grill meat on a barbecue, but that's it. I can't cook to save my life."

"That's reassuring," she declared very seriously.

He opened the top boxes and frowned, clearly puzzled by her statement. He glanced in her direction to invite her to elaborate.

"We wouldn't want you to be perfect, would we?"

Colton laughed while cleaning his hands with the contents of a small bottle of sanitizer.

"No worries about that. If you ask around, you'll be told I have quite a temper."

Her attempt at a mock horror gasp was cut short by his delivering two small plates with mixed greens onto the table accompanied by a bottle of hand cleaning product.

While she opened it and applied it on her hands, he made another trip to the box and returned with two larger plates, each with a large piece of cold salmon covered with dill, with a cream sauce on the side.

"It smells heavenly," Grace commented.

One last trip for butter and, amazingly, bread that was still warm. She tore a piece of it while he sat across from her and poured white wine from a very chilled bottle.

Everything was amazingly delicious.

With anyone else, she would have made a grand statement, something silly like, "I think I'm in love" or "Would you marry me?" but for some reason, Grace couldn't possibly entertain the idea of telling him something like that. Not even in jest. She remained tongue tied and smiled.

The salmon was cooked to perfection. It melted in her mouth, and the seasoning of the salad was perfect.

"This is where the miracle occurs," Colton said with a large gesture of one hand towards the hundreds of wood barrels stored in that part of the building. "The high wine we obtain after the second distillation is poured into those charred oak barrels, and with the barometric pressure, the content of the barrel extends. Water passes through the wood, and the angels take their share."

"Oh, I have heard of the angels' share," she chimed in.

"Good, then you understand that every time we open a barrel, it's a surprise. We don't know if we'll have lost 5, 10, or 50% of its content, but whatever the percentage left, it will have been flavored by the oak."

"How many times can you use a barrel?"

"Just once," he answered. "Think of it as sort of a giant tea bag."

The image was perfect and made her understand the process better. "How long does it have to stay in the barrel to become Bourbon?"

"Legally, there is no minimum period," he explained. "Well, that's for Bourbon. Now, Straight Bourbon is another story. It has to be aged for at least two years. Also, it's not Straight Bourbon if there's anything added."

"What would one add?"

"Coloring, flavoring, or some as unaged neutral grain spirits. Then it's no longer Straight Bourbon but Blended Bourbon."

"And you make?"

"Straight Bourbon, of course," Colton answered. "But mind you, the process doesn't stop with the aging."

"Oh no?"

He shook his head.

"Nope, cause two barrels never taste the same, and people expect a consistent flavor from any given brand, so we have to batch the flavors together to create a uniform product."

"Looks like Bourbon is serious business around here," Grace observed.

"Bourbon and horses. That and pastures. It's our family business. That's what we Greens are all about."

Grace plastered a smile on her face and lowered her eyes to her plate. For the Greens, family was everything.

Their kisses the previous night had made her want to forget it, and she had, just for a while. But twice in the past hour, he had reminded her that she shouldn't.

This was a man most women would dream of. He was not only tall and handsome but also attentive and considerate. He was loyal to his friends and devoted to his family.

Colton had a plan for the future. That plan included a very large house—a house filled with children.

Yes, he was a man with a dream who deserved to see his dream come true and not be saddled with the likes of her.

For the rest of the meal, Grace forced herself to act normally, as if she enjoyed everything, even the splendid chocolate cake they shared.

It was probably delicious, but she had lost her appetite.

Every time she looked up to his kind brown-eyed gaze, it tore something inside of her. His earlier words echoed in her mind.

He wanted to *"be fruitful and multiply,"* and that's one thing she could never do.

CHAPTER 25

COLTON

Something was amiss, and Colton couldn't figure out what.

Despite Mrs. Carson's presence, or maybe because of Mrs. Carson's presence, he'd felt their date had started rather well and continued nicely, but then she pulled away slowly, and then, just before dessert, she completely withdrew.

She was still talking and smiling, but something was gone.

"What is it that triggers your temper?" she asked.

This question surprised him until he remembered he had told her earlier that he had a temper. A very bad one, if one was to ask his brothers.

"So many things, I wouldn't know where to begin. The main one is probably dealing with unfairness."

She tilted her head, inviting him to continue.

"You remember the day you met Gunner for the first time?"

She sat up a little straighter and clutched her napkin.

"Well, that day, I was mad as hell," he continued. "I even stormed into Ashton's office to ask him how he could have possibly decided to favor one of the twins. I even told him that if he felt he should help one of them, then he should have picked Gunner."

Grace's hand flew to her mouth in surprise.

"I would never have guessed it. You seemed so calm when I saw you that day. I imagine Mr. Green explained what we had set out to do."

"No, he didn't. He only told me I was overstepping and, that despite my good intentions, I was actually not acting like a good friend."

"Really?"

"In hindsight, I realize he was most gracious with me that day," Colton confessed. "You see, he showed me that Gunner needed me to trust him and not to be overprotective. Basically, he made me realize that my actions were sabotaging Gunner's self-confidence. If his best friend didn't think him capable of taking care of his own business, then surely his father was right all along when he said that Gunner was good for nothing."

Grace nodded thoughtfully but didn't comment.

"What Ashton didn't tell me was that I was also insulting him."

"How's that?"

"I showed distrust. I imagined the worst and never gave him the benefit of the doubt. That is not acceptable behavior, especially not with a member of my own family." Surprising himself with his own candor, Colton paused and looked at his hands.

"I think I understand what you mean," Grace answered slowly. "However, I also understand that your actions were guided by the best of intentions. You were protecting your friend, and not doing so to belittle him but because you felt he had suffered enough already, and you were afraid we were going to take advantage of him."

He shook his head and remained silent.

"That sort of attitude doesn't make you a bad person," she insisted. "It makes you a knight in shining armor."

"You mean Don Quixote," he answered looking up.

"I'm not so sure. In this case the menace wasn't real, but it didn't come out of nowhere. History had taught you a different story. You know how unfair life had been to your friend. That is why you overreacted."

"Thank you," he said, reaching for her hand across the table.

The gesture startled her, but she didn't pull away.

"You're very welcome," she answered. "You're a good man, Colton Green, a very good man, and I'll consider myself a very lucky girl if you're as good a friend to me as you are to Gunner."

"You want us to be friends?" he asked without bothering to hide the surprise from his voice.

"Yes, that would make me very happy," she answered almost sadly.

Letting go of her hands, he was at a loss for words. Friendship was not what he had in mind at all. He was considering testing a totally different sort of relationship. For some reason — well, because of the previous night—he had thought they were on the same page. How could he have misread her so completely?

"I see," he said, getting up to clear the plates from the table.

"Let me help," she offered.

"No, it's fine. It will only take a minute to put the restaurant plates back in the boxes. The rest can wait until later."

She remained at the table while he quickly put everything away and placed the boxes in the back of his car.

When he closed the trunk, she was standing right beside him with her bag in her hands.

"Shall we go?" she asked.

She seemed so sad and defeated, and Colton just could not figure out why. He hadn't imagined her passion last night. He had felt it. He knew it had been real.

Colton had been sure she was as attracted to him as he was to her, and today she'd left him wondering if he hadn't dreamt the whole thing up.

His legendary temper began to flare.

His mood swung, and now he was mad at her.

Since she had been the one placing them in the friend zone, she had absolutely no right to be sad or upset.

Colton was also mad at himself for getting his hopes up. He should have known better. Still, he opened the door for her but then drove her back to her house in silence with a clenched jaw.

The return trip seemed to last forever. She jumped out of the car before he had a chance to turn off the engine.

She leaned over and put her hand on his arm.

"Thank you, Colton," she whispered. "It was a lovely visit. I had the best time."

She closed the car door and climbed up Mrs. Carson's driveway without looking back. She turned past the corner of the house, and the landlady came out on her door steps to glare at her.

Colton was tempted to linger just to taunt the witch but then decided he had better things to do with his time.

Right, he had dirty plates to deliver to the restaurant and tables to clean up and put away before anyone had a chance to see what a fool he'd made of himself.

CHAPTER 26

GRACE

Grace rushed up the driveway without turning back, eyes glued to the ground, stuck between two angry stares.

She caught the curtain moving from the corner of her eye as she dashed out from Colton's car. She had no doubt her landlady was observing her.

And Colton ... Well, Colton was mad at her, and she couldn't say she blamed him. He had gone out of his way to organize a perfect date, and she had to go and spoil everything by cutting it short.

The irony was that the nicer he was, the more she wanted to push him away. Grace was not a flirty kind of girl, but if she had been, she would never have flirted with Colton. He was too perfect to be played with.

Right that instant, she envied those women who engaged in meaningless teasing. They enjoyed joyous banter which didn't lead to anything. It was a sort of sport for them, a game they played to get reassurance, the kind of comfort a girl could get when she knew she had what it took to capture a man's attention.

On some level, Grace was very flattered by Colton's attitude, but she was too intense to enjoy his kindness and lead him on. If she didn't drive some sort of wedge between them, at least one heart would be broken, and chances were, it was going to be hers—again.

She picked up the key rock, and it was empty. Now, that was weird. Up until then, Mrs. Carson had systematically covered her tracks when she came to inspect the studio. Grace turned the door knob and pushed it open.

"Hello, Gracie, my love," said a too-familiar voice.

"Sam?" Grace took a deep breath to calm down. What she really wanted to do was yell at him to get the hell out of her place, but she didn't.

First, because she didn't want to give Mrs. Carson a reason to come barging in and argue with her that she was in breach of her contract for entertaining a visitor.

Truth be told, he was not a visitor, he was a trespasser, but Grace very much doubted the old lady would see it that way.

Second, because she did not want to give Sam the satisfaction of realizing how annoyed she was with him. The man couldn't seem to comprehend the concept of privacy. He was sitting in her chair in front of her computer, and from the looks of it, he hadn't figured out what her new password was. Grace hoped that frustrated him to no end. It would serve him right for being such a snoop.

"What a surprise," she whispered.

"A good one, I hope," he answered, wiggling his brows.

Grace giggled. At some point in ancient history, when the dinosaurs roamed in Central Park, Grace had thought it adorable when he did that. Right that instant, she saw two furry caterpillars dancing on his brow and making him seem absurdly ridiculous. Grace couldn't stop giggling.

Maybe she had drunk too much wine over lunch.

"What's so funny, my love?"

He moved in her direction with open arms.

She retreated outside of the studio, and he followed her with a puzzled expression on his face.

"You," she said. "Here."

He frowned, and the caterpillars butted heads again.

She fanned herself with her hand and caught her breath. His presence was no laughing matter. He shouldn't be here.

"What are you doing here?" Grace asked.

"Well..." He took another step in her direction, and this time she stood her ground.

"Well what?" There was no trace of mirth in her question.

"I told you the buyer wanted to close on Monday, so I thought the best way to make sure everything was in order was to come and pick up the contract," he answered.

His tone was that of a very smart person finding it tiresome to explain the painfully obvious to a very slow person. Grace analyzed it with a strange detachment.

That sort of answer used to make her feel small. Now, Grace recognized it for what it was—a manipulative ploy to get her to do what he wanted.

"I sent you a revised version of it this morning," Grace said.

"Yes, yes, I know." Sam made exasperated gestures. "I forwarded it to the buyer, and he said his attorneys are good with your changes, so now all you have to do is print it, sign it, and we'll be good to go."

"It's a little bit more complicated than that," Grace said.

"No, it's not," he barked back.

"It sort of is," Grace answer softly. "First, because, as you may have noticed, I do not have a printer at home."

"Oh, right." His tone softened. "What happened to your equipment?"

Most of what Grace owned was in storage, but that was none of his business, so she ignored his question.

"And then the signature needs to be notarized."

"Oh."

The surprise was not feigned. This was a man who loved to think of himself as a plotter but didn't think things through. A very bad combination.

"But surely someone in your office—"

"This is not New York, Sam. This is Elm Ridge, Kentucky."

"Yeah, and?"

"Here people are civilized. Unless there is a real emergency, they don't work on weekends, especially not on the Fourth of July weekend."

"What are we going to do?" he asked. "I need everything signed, sealed, and delivered on Monday in New York."

His arrogance was all gone, and now Grace was faced with a pitiful man. A scared man?

Curiosity was eating her up. Grace would truly have loved to know why he needed the sale to go through on Monday so badly. She understood the offer he presented was good, like ten percent over the market value good, but with a little time, they could probably get a similar one. What made this one so special? She toyed with the idea of asking him and then decided that it was none of her business. He was no longer her husband, and she shouldn't care. The only thing that mattered was taking advantage of the good opportunity to sell.

Deciding that she didn't need to find out what financial jam he had gotten himself into, Grace told him what her plan was.

"*We* are not going to do anything." As she spoke, she moved around so that he was the one outside facing the door while she was standing on the doorstep. "You are going to find yourself a place to spend the night, and you will come back tomorrow at noon."

"Gracie—"

"Let me finish!"

He held his hands up in a surrendering gesture.

"I will return to my office to print the required number of copies of the contract, and then I will endeavor to find someone to notarize my signature for me." Grace was pretty sure that Gloria would do it for her, but until she had made sure and asked her, she was not making any promises. "So, you go about your merry way, and I'll see you tomorrow at noon."

"But Gracie..."

His beaten puppy dog tone didn't move her anymore. As a matter of fact, she found it exasperating.

So much so that she repeated, "Tomorrow at noon." And then slammed the door in his face and leaned against the wall for a minute.

Men!

CHAPTER 27

COLTON

After tossing and turning all night, he felt like an idiot. In the morning light, he couldn't remember what had gotten him so upset.

Colton had played back the scene in his head a hundred times, and while Grace had said she would consider herself lucky if he became her friend, she never said that was all they could ever be.

Even though Colton didn't really know her yet, he was certain that Grace was not the kind of woman who would jump into bed with a total stranger. So maybe, just maybe, what she had meant to say was that she wanted them to get better acquainted before they could become anything else, and like a big oaf, he had taken offense.

Yet, he hadn't withdrawn his invitation to his parents' Sunday barbecue. Looking at his phone he hesitated. Should he text or call to confirm? Should he drive there and apologize for his curt behavior? He opted for a hybrid solution.

Planning to pick you up at noon. Let me know if it's too early.

He waited a minute. No answer. He waited another minute. The phone remained dead. He had another idea.

If you like to swim, pack a bathing suit.

Still no answer. That was… good. It had to be. If she had decided to call it off, she would have texted him back to not bother. Of course, she would have worded it more elegantly, but that still would have been the gist of it.

He tinkered around the house for a bit, glancing at the phone every five minutes. Where was Weston when he needed him? Had he been there, he would made fun of him and would have been very right to do so. Colton scolded himself. He was behaving as if it was his first rodeo.

Except that it was his first rodeo. Grace was not the first woman he had ever been interested in, but there was something different about the attraction he felt for her. He couldn't explain it, but the more he got to know her, the more she grew on him.

When the time came to drive to her place, he was as excited as a teenager on his first date.

Colton was in such a good mood that he even resolved to be pleasant with Mrs. Carson should she step in his way.

She didn't. Good.

He knocked on the door.

"It's open," a man's voice called out. "Come on in."

What the heck?

Colton pushed the door open and stepped in.

Looking around the room, the first thing he noticed was Grace's cell phone on the small table the studio. The table was littered with papers, some of which had fallen to the floor.

Then there was Grace's bed. It looked like a battlefield.

But that was not what shocked him.

What cut his breath out like a sucker punch in the stomach was the fact that there was a man in that bed.

A man who, as far as he could tell, was not wearing a stitch of clothing.

Grace herself was nowhere to be seen. Was she hiding behind the bathroom door?

"Who are you?" they both asked in perfect unison.

They waited a few seconds in silence, and the naked man answered first.

"I'm Sam," he said. "Grace's husband."

"Her husband?"

Colton's mind raced in a thousand different directions.

She had said she was divorced.

She had said it was over.

But maybe it wasn't. Maybe it had been a rough patch.

Maybe her husband realized that he was about to make a big mistake and had asked to be given a second chance?

"Yeah, her husband," he answered with a cocky smile that made Colton want to punch his teeth out. "And Grace and I, well, we're sort of busy right now."

"I see," Colton answered, gritting his teeth.

That was when his phone decided to vibrate in his pocket.

For an instant, he hoped it was Grace texting him back to let him know she would be a bit late. It was absurd since her phone was right in front of him on the table. She couldn't be texting him back.

She was not. It was his mother asking him to pick a quart of milk on his way, as she'd run out.

And now that he had his phone in his hand, he could check out something else. He could make sure that it was Grace's phone he saw in front of him and not *his* phone in an identical blue leather case.

He typed *Hello* and sent the message to Grace's number while staring at the phone on the messy table.

For a few seconds, nothing happened.

His hope rose again.

It was a terrible misunderstanding.

She was sleeping at a friend's house.

That was it. For some reason, she would explain she was lending *him* her studio.

That would be a fun thing to do, just to spite Mrs. Carson.

But then the screen lit up and the phone buzzed.

It was Grace's phone.

Colton needed to get out of there.

He mumbled a "sorry" and rushed away, silently closing the door behind him.

Back in the safety of his car, he banged his head a few times against the steering wheel just to drive some sense into his thick skull.

He was mad as hell.

So, so mad.

Not so much at Grace as at himself.

She had said she wanted them to be friends.

She had been very clear, and if anyone was to blame for a misunderstanding, it was him.

No one else but him.

Except that it was not that simple. She had been sending mixed signals. She had kissed him back. She had held on to him as if her life depended on it. There was so much passion in her embrace, so much fire in her eyes.

He knew he hadn't imagined it. It was all there. It was real. It was real for him, but maybe it wasn't meant for him.

CHAPTER 28

GRACE

"Thank you again," Grace repeated to Gloria as she finished stamping with her notary seal the last copy of the sales contract.

"Don't mention it," she said. "You actually saved me from some very tedious chore my mother reserves for Sunday mornings."

"Well, in that case," Grace said, "let me know if there's anything I can do to make it up to her."

Gloria laughed. It was a sad laugh though.

"No, unfortunately, there's not much anyone can do for her these days. She's just a shadow of her former self, and her grasp on the world is getting thinner with every passing month."

"I'm so sorry."

"Don't be," she said with a real smile. "She's lived a full life, a very rich one, and she's still loved and taken care of, so it's all good."

She had a hundred questions for Gloria. Did her mother live with her? Who took care of her when she was at work?

How did she cope with the degradation of her mother's condition? But Gloria was such a private person, Grace was afraid to ask.

It was one of those tricky situations that Grace hated. Those who asked too many questions seemed to suffer from some form of morbid curiosity, while those who didn't ask anything were considered as lacking compassion.

She rested a hand on Gloria's arm and said, "Just remember, this is a two-way street."

"I know. And I'm also serious when I tell you that you saved my morning. There's one thing that is like an anchor in my mother's mind: Sunday after church is when we clean the copper pots."

"Lemon and salt?" Grace asked.

"How did you know?" Gloria's surprise was genuine.

"My mother had a love affair with those pots when I was a kid," she explained.

"Then you know why I was grateful to escape."

They sorted the pages and stapled the documents in silence for a bit until Grace decided to confide in her.

"When Sam called me to tell me he had a buyer for our place, I was annoyed. The plan had been to keep the apartment for a few more years, as real estate in Manhattan is always a good investment."

"You're right," Gloria admitted. "I can't believe someone would be ready to pay so much money for a one-bedroom place."

Pulling out a large manila envelope from a drawer, she mumbled, "city people" as if living in a large city was a perfect explanation for all sort of strange behaviors.

She stacked all the copies but one into the envelope and looked at Grace again.

"And now that it's almost done, how do you feel?"

"Relieved," she confessed. "Like I've completely turned the page."

"Good. And let me tell you, if you want to reinvest the proceeds of the sales in Elm Ridge, I will help you find a nice not-so-little house in our neck of the woods."

She sounded as if her staying here was a done deal. It wasn't. Ashton Green had yet to tell her he wanted her to stay past her test period. Yet she played along.

"You would? That would be amazing, because I wouldn't know where to start with a house."

"I'll teach you all I know, and then we'll find you a good inspector and..." she looked at Grace and laughed, a real honest to God laugh this time, "I know I get really excited about house shopping. Some days I think I've missed my calling. I should have been a realtor."

"That's the best excuse there is to look at real estate porn all day," Grace agreed.

They left the office, and while she entered her car, Grace heard Gloria chuckle. Talking to herself she said, "Real estate *porn*? What I watch is called real estate porn, who knew?"

With a lighter heart, Grace drove back to Mrs. Carson's place, and just as she parked on the street, a large black SUV drove away. It made her think of Colton. Actually, everything made her think of Colton.

The funniest thing was that Sam of all people was the one who made her think about Colton the most. When she compared the two of them, she wondered how she had ever managed to fall in love with Sam.

She couldn't identify Sam's rental car because some of the neighbors were having guests for the weekend, and there were more cars than usual. Yet she had no doubt he was already there and ready to run with the documents.

Why was she not surprised he was not waiting by the door

as she had asked him to? The white key rock was upside down and her door ajar. She cursed herself for not thinking about taking the key with her. Not that she had anything to hide, but she should have kept him out just to teach him a lesson.

But then again, she wasn't thinking straight that morning when she'd left to meet with Gloria. She had even left her phone behind. She hadn't done that in ages. Actually, she hadn't done that since they had separated. Hmm, that was interesting.

Pushing the door open, she couldn't believe her eyes!

"What the heck are you doing in my bed?" she screamed.

"What do you think," he asked, wiggling his brows at her.

"And what are you doing with my phone?"

"Gracie..." he cooed, putting it on the floor and motioning for her to come sit next to him on the bed.

"Don't Gracie me, mister," she barked. "You've got a baby on the way. The only woman you should think of lying next to is the mother of your child."

"Well, about that," he said with a sheepish look. "She lied to me. She wasn't pregnant."

"And so what?"

"Don't you see? There was no reason for us to end our marriage. It changes everything!"

"No, it doesn't." How could he possibly think it would? "What changed everything was the fact that you could have entertained the possibility that she was expecting a child of yours."

"Gracie..." he purred.

"You have thirty seconds to get your sorry behind out of my bed and out of my place. After that, I will tear this envelope up and you can kiss your sale goodbye!"

He hesitated and seemed to consider calling her bluff until she started counting.

"Thirty, twenty-nine, twenty-eight... "

He jumped out of bed and put his pants back on.

"Twenty-seven, twenty-six, twenty-five..."

He looked for his socks and shoes under the bed.

"Twenty-four, twenty-three, twenty-two..."

He found his shirt and his jacket.

"Twenty-one, twenty, nineteen..."

"You're crazy, you know," he said, standing in front of her. "Absolutely certifiable!"

"Eighteen, seventeen, sixteen..."

He tore the envelope away from her hand and dashed for the door, but he couldn't open it since both of his hands were full.

Taking mercy on him, she opened the door for him while continuing to count.

"Fifteen, fourteen, thirteen..."

Sam ran out and—rats—bumped into Mrs. Carson, who stared at him as if he was a madman. Grace couldn't blame her since he did look a bit crazed—shirtless, his shoes and socks in one hand, his shirt, tie, and suit jacket in the other, and the envelope tucked under his arm.

"Have a safe trip back," she called out to his back as he ran out along the driveway without looking behind him. Turning to her landlady, she asked, "What can I do for you, Mrs. Carson?"

"Move out," she said.

"When?" Grace asked.

The question surprised her, and she almost looked disappointed. Was she looking forward to a fight? Grace was not. Sam had knocked the wind off her sails.

"Tomorrow?" she suggested.

"And what about today, and I don't pay any of the July rent?"

Mrs. Carson paused to think about it for a minute and nodded.

"That would be just fine."

Well, finally that was something they could agree on.

CHAPTER 29

GRACE

Grace paced, wondering what to do. She should be in a festive mood.

Finally, she was out of Mrs. Carson's sad place and into a cozy little log cabin. It was possibly a bit too isolated for her taste, but it was cheap and only twenty minutes away from work. When she first entered the living room, she had wanted to squeal with delight. She loved how rustic and quaint it was.

And if her Sunday move wasn't cool enough, she had gotten even better news on Monday. Her last tie to Sam had been severed. The money would be in the bank later in the week, and she would never have to talk to him again for the rest of her life.

Everything was going her way. It truly was.

Ever since she and Sam had separated, life had been good to her. She should have been dancing with joy and looking forward to the big party she was invited to.

All the members of the firm and their families were attending Ashton Green's party. The celebration was the only thing people had been talking about all week, and there she was moping, chased by her old demons tempting her with visions of quiet reading on the balcony hammock.

She needed to go there. It would look really bad if she was the only one to not come. The least she could do was make an appearance. Right, she didn't have to stay long, but if she wanted to become a real member of the team, she needed to spend time with her coworkers.

Armed with a strong resolve, she drove back to Elm Ridge and surprised herself. It hadn't been that long since she'd arrived, but she was starting to find her way around without fear of losing her GPS signal.

If she were to judge by the number of cars parked along the road, the crowd was larger than on Memorial Day. Had Ashton Green invited the entire town? He very well could have.

She parked at some distance and doubled back on foot. She breathed in the delicious grilled meat smell and remembered this was where she'd seen Colton for the first time. She was disappointed to not see him at the giant barbecue grill. Audrey and Cora were manning the fire while the twins, Elisabeth and Faith, were running back and forth bringing the burgers and steaks to the guests.

"Hey there," Audrey called out when she noticed her.

"Hello, sorry I'm late," Grace apologized.

Cora scolded her with her best stern old fashion school teacher voice imitation, "Now, you listen, young lady, today is a holiday. There's no schedule, no timetable, just good clean fun."

"Yes, ma'am," she answered with a mock salute.

"So, what will you have?" Audrey asked.

"I'm not sure yet," she told her. "Maybe I'll start with a salad."

Audrey and Cora laughed. Now, how was that funny?

Noticing her surprise, Audrey explained, "Bailey and Willow had a heated discussion over the salads."

"Oh, that must have been interesting," Grace said. "Did the chef and the nutritionist find a middle ground?"

"Not exactly," Cora answered with a mischievous smile.

"What she means is Bailey won," Audrey clarified.

Grace bit her lips to keep from cheering and appearing unsupportive of Willow.

That would be mean, but the fact was, she did like some seasoning in her salads. Willow meant well. Grace knew where Willow was coming from. She was fighting the good fight against cholesterol, and she admired her for it. However, today was not the day for educating the crowd about healthy nutrition. If she tried, her words would fall on deaf ears.

Moving away from the grill, Grace approached the buffet tables and chatted with a few people she knew. From the corner of her eye, she spotted three of the Green brothers in a crowd of dancers on a makeshift dance floor. She moved closer to get a better look.

Where the singer would stand in a regular band, there was a man, mike in hand, talking so fast she couldn't understand half of what he was saying.

"He's the caller," Ashton Green explained as he came to stand next to her.

"A caller?"

"A caller is the person who prompts the dance figures in square dancing."

"You mean he tells them what to do?"

"That's right."

And now that she was paying attention, Grace noticed that indeed, the dancers did follow some sort of direction as the man with the microphone, the caller, issued his orders.

Up to that very moment, she'd just assumed people always

did the same thing in the same order. Obviously now, she understood it was not so.

The caller shouted *Courtesy Turn,* and all the women put their left hand in the left hand of one of the men, and somehow the men's right hands landed on the women's right hands they had previously placed on the small of their backs. He called *Wrong Way Grand,* and dancers changed partners, taking one left hand and one right hand alternatively.

"It's clean fun and good exercise too," Ashton said.

To her, it appeared too complicated to be any sort of fun. She would be terrified of stepping on another dancer's toes.

One of the woman dancers caught her eye. Her blond hair flowed around her as she effortlessly passed from one man to another and ended up—in Colton's arms.

The music stopped, and the two of them walked away from the dance floor. The blond beauty wrapped an arm along his waist as she had when they danced, and he laughed at something she said while they settled by the bar. They were standing at some distance but right in front of her. Colton looked in her direction, and she smiled at him.

He didn't smile back. He acted as if he didn't see her.

He poured water from a frosted pitcher into two glasses and turned around to give one to his dancing partner. She stood on tiptoes and gave him a quick kiss. It landed on one corner of his lips.

Grace's heart skipped a beat, and she cursed herself.

She was overreacting. It didn't mean a thing. Colton hadn't prompted it. But even if he had, it was fine. She was a fine-looking young lady, and he was a free man.

But no. It was just a thank you kiss that landed there by accident—unless it was more. Grace scolded herself. She was going crazy.

She was about to turn around when Colton looked in her

direction again. He still didn't smile, but this time he acknowledged her presence with a small tilt of his head.

The message was loud and clear. She had had her chance, and she had let it pass. He'd moved on.

A smile only returned to his lips when he turned towards the blond beauty who had finished her glass. They seemed so easy with each other that it hurt.

It hurt almost as bad as when Sam had announced that he was leaving her because another woman was going to turn him into a dad.

It hurt as bad, but it didn't hurt the same...

Grace didn't have time to dwell upon it, as Ashton Green had kept talking to her. The problem was she hadn't heard a word he'd said. She quickly caught up when she heard the end of his sentence.

"—we can draft the new contract tomorrow," he said, looking at her expectantly. "And I'll be happy to announce to everyone right away that you're a permanent addition to our firm."

"Could we not do it today?" she asked.

Ashton frowned. "Of course." His tone was still friendly, but now that she knew him better, she saw he was upset. Maybe not upset. More like disappointed or surprised. He had every right to feel that way since she had told him only a few days ago that she was sold on staying and would be delighted to be an official part of his team.

How could he understand her request to postpone his announcement when she didn't even understand it herself?

"You're having second thoughts?" he asked.

Grace skirted the issue.

"Will you give me one more night to sleep on it?"

"Absolutely," he answered a bit abruptly. "Now if you'll excuse me."

"Of course."

He walked away to greet some new guests. Grace looked around and wondered what to do next. She needed some alone time to think.

The caller announced the next dance, and blondie pulled Colton by the hand in the direction of the dance floor. Wearing an amused smile on his lips, he didn't see anyone but her.

The band began to play again, and Grace took it as her cue to leave. Yes, it was time to go home. Home alone. Well almost. There was a green monster sitting on her shoulder and shredding her heart to pieces.

She needed to figure it out. Had that man managed to steal her heart? If he had, could she stick around and watch him be happy with another woman?

Probably not. It was absurd, but maybe the best thing for her could be to pick herself up and try fresh again somewhere else.

CHAPTER 30

COLTON

The band stopped to take another break, and Sandy called out to her daughter from the table nearest to the dance floor.

"Chrissie Ball, come and spend some time with your mother!"

Grateful for the interruption because there was only so much dancing he could take, Colton accompanied the little minx to the table, and after saluting Doctor Nayar, he was drafted by Gloria to help her bring some burgers to the table.

Sandy had twisted her ankle and was milking her injured status all she could. The woman loved to be the center of attention.

Happy to have a chance to escape from her clutches, Colton followed Gloria, who seemed to be searching for someone.

"Have you seen Grace?" she asked.

"I did earlier when we were dancing," Colton answered. "She was talking with Ashton."

"I know," she said. "That's why I'm looking for her. Ashton told me he has offered her a permanent position, and she's asked for time to think about it."

"I can't say I'm surprised."

Gloria stopped and frowned at him.

"Why do you say that?"

"Because I think she's a city girl at heart."

"That doesn't make sense," Gloria said. "Just a few days ago, she was telling me how much she loves it here and how her quality of life has increased since she's moved to Elm Ridge."

"Then maybe she and her husband reconciled?"

Colton wasn't proud of fishing for information in that way, but he was a sucker for punishment. He wanted to know what had happened.

Gloria laughed as if his question was the most absurd thing she'd ever heard. "Nope," she said adamantly, resuming her walk toward the barbecue with Colton in tow. "If there's one thing I know for sure it's that they didn't reconcile."

"Well, I did run into the man in Elm Ridge," Colton replied. "Why else would he come here if not to woo her back?"

Gloria stopped abruptly again and gave him a hard look.

"Jealous?" she asked.

He shrugged away her question.

"Oh, my Lord, you *are* jealous," she whispered.

She looked around them checking to see if they were within ear's reach of the nearest group of guests and leaned toward him.

"You're right," she said softly. "The man did show up in Elm Ridge on Saturday, but it was not to woo her back, as you so gently put it. It was to get her to sign some papers."

Observing his expression, Gloria seemed to hesitate and then decided to tell him more to convince him.

"Now, I'll have to grant you that he did try to talk her into a roll in the hay, you know, for old times' sake, but she sent him packing."

"How do you know that?"

"Well, on Sunday morning, she and I met at the firm to notarize copies of a sale contract, and she called me back an hour later to ask if I had a realtor to recommend."

Colton made a face to indicate that what she was saying didn't make any sense at all.

"Can you imagine, the man had found a way to get into her place and was waiting for her, in her home," her voice dropped down even lower when she added, "in her bed in nothing but his birthday suit."

Yes, that Colton could imagine because he had seen it with his own two eyes. Yet, he was not about to tell her that.

"She sent him packing so quickly that he ran out of the house with only his pants on!" She laughed. "I would have paid good money to see that, especially when he ran right into Mrs. Carson."

That must have indeed been an interesting encounter.

"Of course, that didn't go well at all with the old lady. She always insisted on having provision in the lease that specified her tenants are not allowed to have visitors."

The pieces of the puzzle started to fall into place.

Just to make sure, Colton asked Gloria, "Mrs. Carson asked her to leave? Was that why she needed a realtor?"

"Yes, Grace wanted to move out as soon as possible," Gloria explained. "I haven't spoken to her since."

"Who did you recommend?" he asked.

"I told her we would talk about it on Wednesday at the office, but for now, she should look at the vacation rentals by owner sites," she said. "There are plenty of cottages you can get for a week during the summer. I figured she would find one to tide her over while she looked for another place."

"Good idea."

"Right." Gloria seemed rather pleased with herself for coming up with that solution. "I thought that now she's sold her New York apartment, she will have enough to put a down payment on a house in Elm Ridge and become a permanent part of our lives."

They had arrived at the barbecue, and Gloria asked Audrey, "Did you see Grace?"

"I did see her when she got here a while back, but I haven't seen her since."

Arriving with a clean stack of plates, Elisabeth overheard the conversation and said, "I think she's left already."

"She did?" Gloria asked.

"Yes," Elisabeth confirmed. "I thought it was rather odd, as she'd just arrived, but she seemed upset, you know, as if she was about to cry."

"And you didn't go to her?" Audrey asked.

"I almost did, but I didn't dare stop her. I hardly know her," Elisabeth answered a bit defensively. "It would have been strange if I had because I must have seen her what, twice in my life? I didn't want to pry."

Gloria put a comforting hand on Elisabeth's arm and told her she did the right thing. Elisabeth seemed relieved.

She was such a gentle soul that it would probably have haunted her for the rest of the day if she'd thought she had done wrong by Grace by letting her walk away without offering comfort.

"I agree with Gloria," Colton chimed in.

Audrey softened and apologized for being abrupt with her sister. "Of course, I'm sorry Elisabeth. I didn't mean to snap at you. It's just that now I'm worried about her."

"Well, we'll just need to call her," Gloria said, pulling her phone out of her back pocket.

They all looked at her while she dialed Grace's number and waited with the phone on her ear.

"Hey, Grace," she said. "It's Gloria. Please call me back when you get this message."

She put the phone back in her pocket and told them what they had all guessed. "It went straight to voice mail."

"Maybe she cuts it off when she drives," Elisabeth offered.

Or maybe she didn't want to talk to anyone today.

Elisabeth was very observant, so if she said Grace looked upset, something must have been troubling her. And now Colton was starting to wonder if it was his fault. Could it be because he made a point of ignoring her earlier while being very affectionate with Chrissie?

The idea that Grace could have reacted that way to his attitude and that she could actually be jealous brought up mixed feelings.

On one hand, it perversely made him very happy because it meant that despite her pushing him away, she did care about him. On the other hand, he felt somehow offended. Grace should have known better than that. Chrissie was a kid. It was plain that Sandy's daughter was barely legal for goodness sake! As if it was his style to rob the cradle. No. Chrissie was dating material for his kid brother.

Jaxon came storming in Colton's direction, growling into his cell phone, "So that's it? You're leaving me hanging?"

Whomever he was talking to must have cut the conversation short because he stared at his cell phone screen for a second in disbelief..

"Something wrong?" It was a dumb question, but what else could Colton say.

"The cook just quit," Jaxon tucked the phone away in his back pocket. "I've got ten kids arriving on Monday and double that the following week, and no one to cook for them."

"Time to pull out the Betty Crocker cookbook," he teased.

Jaxon was not amused. "I'd better go find a quiet spot to make some phone calls."

"Good luck," Colton called after him. His brother wasn't the only one who needed to straighten out a few things. He needed to find Grace and apologize for being an ass. Fast.

Colton helped Gloria bring some plates back to her table and excused himself. He needed to find Grace.

Ten minutes later, he was at Mrs. Carson's place, and Grace's small car was nowhere to be seen.

Still, just to be sure, he decided to go knock on her door.

Mrs. Carson didn't give him a chance to do so. A few seconds after he opened his car door, she was in his way.

"What are you doing here?" she asked rather testily.

"I've come to call on Ms. Baker," Colton answered.

"Then you've come to the wrong address," she answered with a sneer. "She moved out on Saturday."

Colton hated to have to ask her for anything, but he had no choice. She was his only lead. "Would you, by any chance, know where she has moved?"

With obvious satisfaction, she shook her head. "I didn't ask."

"Well, thank you for your help," he said before turning around to leave.

The irony of his answer seemed to fly way over her head, as she was lost in her own train of thought.

She snapped out of it and called out after him.

"I do not want anything to do with the likes of her or you, if I can help it. You two deserve each other!"

That last sentence brought a smile to his face.

Maybe she was on to something.

CHAPTER 31

GRACE

Finding her way back to the cabin, Grace realized that July 4th was serious business around Elm Ridge. The place was like a ghost town. Aside from the gas station, she hadn't seen a single shop open.

It was such a different life from the one she was living only a couple of months earlier that she had to stop and ask herself again if she was ready to settle.

Of course, growing new roots here would mean foregoing a lot of opportunities she had in New York. But, the fact was, she never took advantage of those opportunities.

Thinking back, she could count on the fingers of one hand the number of times she'd gone to the theater in the past five years. She'd been too busy working to take the time to go to a show or visit a museum. She didn't even go to the movies!

In hindsight, it was clear work had been her entire life. She'd had no time for anything else.

Maybe that was what had driven Sam away. Maybe she was also to the blame for the death of their marriage.

She hadn't cheated on him, but she had not invested enough time to keep the relationship afloat either. Sam was right when he said she was a rat trapped in a maze of her own choosing. Would she miss that? Certainly not.

Her income had taken a serious nosedive since she'd moved, but then again, she hadn't really taken advantage of the money she made before. Between her student loans and the cost of living in Manhattan, money vanished far too quickly.

If she stayed here, her quality of life would not suffer because of the drop in income.

She'd had this discussion with herself a hundred times, and the scale tipped largely in favor of Elm Ridge.

So why was she hesitating?

Why hadn't she jumped with joy and accepted Ashton Green's offer right away?

Why? When she took a hard look at herself, she knew why.

She could put a name to the reason that made her hesitate.

That name was Colton.

She didn't think it possible, at least not for her, but now she knew better. It was possible to fall for a man in a few weeks. It was possible even though she actually didn't know who he truly was. For instance, he had confessed that he had a temper, but if he hadn't said it, she would never have guessed.

What else did she not know about him?

Had she fallen in love with him or with what she imagined him to be? And was what she imagined him to be close to reality?

She had no clue.

What Grace knew, however, was the pain she'd felt when he had ignored her earlier, and that pain scared her so much that she wanted to run away.

For all Grace knew, he could be nearsighted. He could have lost his contact lenses and not seen her at a distance, except that he did see her a minute later.

There was no denying it. The sole reason why she was wavering about her future in Elm Ridge was her fear of feeling that pain again every time she saw him.

It was such a close-knit community that she would necessarily run into him periodically, and the very idea of watching him fall in love with another woman made her sick.

She parked by her small cabin and remained in her car for a minute thinking hard until she came to the only possible conclusion: she had to move away.

She wasn't enough of a masochist to stay and watch the unavoidable happen. Sooner or later, Colton Green would find the perfect woman. A woman who didn't have a past. A woman who would be happy to become a part of the Green clan and give him half a dozen kids who would run around his dream house on the hill and grow up with their numerous first and second cousins.

As she left the car to settle on the outside swing where she'd left her book earlier, she resolved to convince herself that this sort of life wasn't for her.

Coming from a family of two, she would never adjust to becoming a member of such a big tribe. Just off the top of her head she could name nineteen members of that clan. As soon as Ashton's daughters and Colton's siblings found spouses and start their own families, one would actually need a cheat sheet to remember who was who.

Yes, she did need to go.

There were thousands of human-size law firms in hundreds of small towns. There was a world of opportunities open to her.

She was going to be fine.

She knew it with certainty.

Yet, this knowledge didn't help her at all right then.

Picking up her book, she attempted to concentrate on the

engaging story that had captured her imagination earlier. It was so much fun to live vicariously along with some wild romantic adventures on paper or shed tears of sorrow over a fictitious heartbreak.

Except that today it didn't seem to work.

There was something distracting her.

It took her a good minute to understand what it was—the constant buzz of her phone vibrating against the loose change at the bottom of her purse.

Grace fished it out of the bag and gasped at the numbers on the screen.

Either she was the most popular girl in town, or something horrible had happened.

She checked the origin of the calls: Gloria, Audrey, Willow, Gloria again, and then Colton. There was only one voice mail. It was from Gloria briefly asking her to return her call.

There were five text messages.

It started with Audrey: *Where did you go? Is everything ok?*

And continued with Willow: *Hey girl, where are you hiding?*

And then Colton.

Way too many messages.

She hesitated.

The smart thing to do would be to erase them, to make them disappear without reading a single word.

Yes, that would be smart, and most of the time she was actually a smart girl.

She was.

Except where men were concerned.

CHAPTER 32

COLTON

"Where have you been?" Colton's mother asked when he returned to the party. "Ashton was looking all over for you."

"I had an errand to run."

His mother's eyebrows shot to the sky, but she refrained from asking any further questions. Instead, she directed him to the kitchen where Ashton was arbitrating some sort of minor crisis for which his help was required.

That tickled his curiosity.

Nevertheless, he took the long route to the back of the house to avoid passing by Sandy's table and getting drafted into another round of dancing with Chrissie. He'd done his good deed for the day.

He pushed open the kitchen door that had been left ajar. The lights were off, and the room was perfectly silent. Oh well, the crisis had been resolved without him.

He was about to turn around and leave when he heard his uncle say, "Hey there," with a hoarse voice. "Come on in, but don't turn on the light."

Uh-oh. Now he got it.

Ashton was getting one of his legendary migraines.

"How bad is it?" Colton asked.

"I've had worse," he answered. "I've taken my meds, but they don't seem to kick in as fast as I want them to."

"What can I do?"

"First, help me get to bed."

He stood from the kitchen wooden bench, a pouch of ice in hand, and wobbled like a drunken sailor. Colton was by his side holding him before he had a chance to fall.

It was not clear if it was the migraine or the medication, but when he took his drugs, he did act as if he had had a too much to drink.

"Okay, I got you," Colton said, helping him make his way out of the kitchen. "Your den or the bedroom?"

"Den."

That was easier. The den was on the other side of the house, while his bedroom was up a flight of stairs.

"Should I call Dr. Nayar?" Colton asked as he helped him lie on his back on the daybed in his home office.

"Nah," Ashton said, putting the ice on his forehead. "But I may need you to help Landon handle the fireworks. He assisted me when I set them up, and it's a two man job. Even if I feel better in an hour, I won't be able to deal with the noise."

"Sure, no problem," Colton answered, pulling the drapes shut to make the room as dark as possible. "I'll find Dad and we'll figure it out."

"You're a good boy Colton," Ashton whispered.

The younger man couldn't help but laugh. When he was in his fifties, he would still be a boy to his uncle.

"Thanks, Uncle Ashton."

"I mean it. I really do, and not a week goes by without my cursing myself for not fighting harder for you."

That stopped Colton dead in his tracks.

"I wanted to be the one to adopt you, you know, but Julia

wouldn't hear of it. She said that no matter how much she loved or trusted Addison and me, no one but her was going to raise her sister's son."

Colton was speechless.

He knew he was adopted. He had always known that. But no one had ever told him about Ashton's attempt to take him in. If not for the drugs in his uncle's system, Ashton might have gone to his grave without ever mentioning it.

Leaning against the wall, Colton stopped to digest the information. What would his life have been like if Ashton had had his way?

Sophia would have had five brothers instead of six, and he would have had six sisters instead of one. Would they have told him about it from the start as his parents had?

It was an alternate reality he could barely imagine.

"You get some rest now," Colton said before softly closing the door behind him. He silently made his way back to the kitchen where he found the twins eating ice cream at the kitchen table and giggling as young girls should.

"Hey, Colton," Faith said when she noticed him. "What's up?"

"Your Dad's trying to nap in his den," he answered. "He's asked me to take over the fireworks. Would you young ladies like to help me with that?"

Faith opened and closed her mouth like a landed fish while Elisabeth turned around and said, "You're serious?"

He nodded.

"Oh, Colton, you're the best!" she squealed, jumping into his arms.

Shushing her, he hugged her back.

"Ooops," she whispered, looking contrite, "I almost forgot about Dad!"

From the look on their faces, Colton imagined they were

struggling with mixed feelings. On one hand, they were sorry to see their father miss out on his favorite party of the year, but on the other hand, they were delighted to have a chance to play with fire.

Ashton was so protective of his daughters that he never let them participate in his fireworks preparation. Colton, on the other hand, thought he should teach them like Landon had taught Weston and him. He would have taught Jaxon had he shown any interest.

Ashton had taught every single one of his daughters how to handle a gun, so there was no reason for him not to share his love of pyrotechnics with them as well.

"Don't you dare tell anyone about it before it's done," Colton warned them. If Addison found out, she would have a puppy.

"Mum's the word," Faith said, almost hopping up and down with impatience.

"Then I'll see you in the clearing in an hour."

Colton abandoned them to go search for his father. On his way, he pulled out his phone to check for messages and bumped into Willow who was also looking at her phone.

They both laughed and apologized.

"Have you seen Grace?" Colton asked. "I caught a glimpse of her for a minute and then she vanished."

"I have no idea where she went," Willow answered. "I was texting her. I'm wondering if she didn't go back to her place."

"I heard she moved. Did you know?"

"Sure. I even helped her. Not that she had so much to pack, but she was happy for company to go pick a place."

"And she found something right away?"

"Oh, yes, she got really lucky. There was a last-minute cancellation, so she got a very pretty cabin for a week at a discounted price. It's actually very close to your distillery, and it's the cutest place ever," Willow explained with a dreamy smile. "It's got a wraparound deck with a big swing under a mosquito net. Yeah, it's like a tree house for grownups."

And now it was his turn to smile because he knew precisely what cabin Willow was talking about. Thanks to her, he had an address to zoom to as soon as he was done with the fireworks.

CHAPTER 33

GRACE

The sound of the fireworks startled Grace out of her daydreaming.

The sky flickered in the distance.

Was it Ashton's handy work?

She should have stayed.

The man went out of his way to throw a huge party like that, and she had run away to throw herself a miserable self-pity one.

She was way too selfish and absurdly oversensitive.

There was no reason for her to get so upset simply because Colton was dancing with another girl. But then again, he didn't just dance with her, he had pointedly ignored Grace when they made eye contact.

Boohoo, he ignored me. When had she become so childish?

She kept blaming Sam, but shouldn't she blame herself for letting him bring her down?

Grace got lost in her thoughts staring at the sky long after the fireworks ended. The wonderfully starlit sky was enough to capture her attention. That was until the beams of a car's head-lights illuminated her driveway.

Her heart raced. She shut out the outside lamps and looked for a place to hide.

Why had she even considered renting a place like this in the middle of nowhere? Was she crazy? Mrs. Carson's place was far from perfect, but at least it wasn't isolated. If someone had broken in the studio or if she had started screaming in the middle of the night, the old lady would have come to her doorstep with the shotgun that hung in her hallway. She had showed it to her when she first moved in, telling her she knew how to use it, and strangely enough, Grace had found it reassuring.

What was she thinking?

The driver stopped and left the car lights on.

"Grace," he called out.

"Colton?" she shouted back, switching the lights back on. "Colton is that you? You scared the hell out of me!"

He ran up the steps and was by her side in an instant.

"I texted I was on my way," he said.

She looked down to the phone on the table by the swing and the blinking lights did confirm that indeed, she had more unread messages.

His gaze followed hers.

"You would know if you answered your phone or looked at your messages," he said coming closer yet.

She nodded silently.

"Are you shaking?" he asked.

"Yes, I guess." There was no denying it. "Your arrival took me by surprise."

He took her in his arms and whispered, "A city girl like you shouldn't stay by herself in the middle of the woods."

"You're probably right," she conceded, leaning against him.

His warmth was comforting, and when he gently pushed

her hair away from her face to kiss her, all her resolve to stay away from him melted away.

When he broke the kiss, she was shaking harder, but it was not from fear anymore.

"Why did you leave the party?" he asked, pulling her with him on the swing.

"It's complicated," she lied.

"I have all the time in the world," he said wrapping one arm around her.

She rested her head on his shoulder and wondered where to begin.

"What about if I go first?" he suggested.

"Okay," she agreed with relief.

"I really care for you, Grace. I think you like me too."

He paused and she remained silent.

He hadn't asked but stated a fact. An obvious one too. Of course, she liked him. He was right. If she didn't, she would not have kissed him, would she?

"At times, I'm certain you do, but then you pull away and I can't figure out why," he continued. "And since we're past the age of playing games, I figured I would ask you why."

He lifted her face up toward his with a finger under her chin and looked into her eyes.

"Talk to me, Grace," he asked before dropping a light kiss on her lips.

She took a big breath and looked away. It would be easier if she didn't look at him.

"I do care for you, Colton," she confessed. "A lot more than I ever thought possible after such a short time."

"But… Obviously, there's a but," he said, pulling her closer so that her head rested against his shoulder again.

"But… I don't think you're a player."

"You're right, I am not."

"And I don't think you and I, you know, if it got serious... Well, I don't think it would work."

"I gathered that much. What I don't understand is why," he answered sweetly.

"Because we're too different," Grace said.

She felt him sigh and decided the direct way was the best way.

"You have a family," she explained. "A real one, where people love and support each other. Of course, I am realistic, I imagine there has to be arguments and disagreements at times, but somehow you always manage to make it work because in your world, family does come first."

"It does," he agreed. "But why is that a problem?"

"Because I come from a totally different world. I told you, I never had a family. I'm the child of a single mom, a child without a father, without uncles, aunts, and cousins. I'm not used to sharing my life with so many people, and furthermore—"

She hesitated, and he remained silent, giving her time, waiting for her to continue.

"Also, I have a past. I mean, I'm divorced..."

"And so what?" he interrupted. "I know you were married before, and it's no big deal. This is the 21st century after all. I do have traditional values, but I didn't expect to marry a virgin."

"Let me finish please," she pleaded.

"Sorry," he said patting her hair gently. "Please continue, but let me tell you, counselor, that so far you haven't made your case."

That's because she'd kept the worst news for last.

Just thinking about it brought tears to her eyes. She took another big breath and attempted to sit up away from him.

He didn't let her and kept her pressing against his side.

"Come on, Grace," he said. "I don't think there's anything you could tell me that could change the way I feel about you."

She breathed him in one last time and braced herself for her final confession.

CHAPTER 34

COLTON

Grace was struggling.

All the reasons she'd been giving him so far were just excuses.

Why would she think for a minute that they couldn't be a good match because she came from a family of two whereas his was so big that he'd given up on keeping count?

This didn't make sense.

There were hundreds of things Colton ignored about her, but that was fine. Discovering them was something he was looking forward to.

He was certain she was not hiding some nefarious secret past, first and foremost because he trusted his instincts and his gut told him she was a good person.

Second, because the very fact that Ashton asked her to join his firm confirmed his analysis. They were both good enough judges of character. Furthermore, Ashton had certainly run a thorough background check on her, and obviously, he hadn't uncovered any dark secrets.

Whatever it was, he was sure they could work it out.

That is, if she wanted to.

"You remember when we went out and I first told you about my husband?" she asked.

"Ex-husband," he corrected her.

"Right, ex-husband," she rephrased. "And you asked me why I didn't consider fighting to fix my marriage."

"That was rude of me, and I apologize for it," Colton said.

"No, no, don't apologize. I understand you didn't mean to be judgmental. You were curious about why I wouldn't do what you considered to be the proper thing to do given your family history."

She did have a point. Even though his parents always kept their disagreements private, especially when the kids were young, everyone had noticed when they had gone through a rough patch. They all feared for the worst a bit back then, but his parents had figured it out. That was what people did in the Green family.

"Well, there was a reason I didn't fight," she continued. "It's because he had told me the new woman in his life was giving him something I had been unable to give him."

She swallowed hard, and her voice was just a whisper when she finished her sentence.

"She had told him she was expecting."

That did change everything. How could it not?

Especially for her, who was the daughter of an unknown father. Of course, she would think the right thing to do was to walk away gracefully.

Why would she think that he would hold that against her?

"He said it showed how damaged I was."

"What?" It was hard for Colton to contain his rage. What a miserable human being that man was. Not only did he cheat on his wife big time and obviously without protection, but he also felt the need to insult her?

"Yeah, because we'd been trying for years and she, well, she got the baby started right away." She let out a sad little laugh and added, "Or so he thought."

"She wasn't really pregnant?"

Somehow that made him happy. That idiot fell for the oldest trick in the book, and it served him right. At least something good came out of it. Grace was freed from a bad partner.

"Nope. At least that's what he told me when he came to get the closing papers," Grace said.

"Is the sale final?" Colton asked.

"Yep. Signed, sealed, and delivered."

"Good. Then you have no reason to go back to New York."

She shook her head and then looked up at him. "You and I can't work because you'll want to start your own family and I, well I can't have kids, Colton."

All the sadness in the world transpired in that last sentence.

"Have you ever heard of adoption?" he asked softly.

She smiled and looked away again. "That's such a sweet thing to say. I know you are sincere, but wouldn't you rather have your own?"

"When you adopt a child, he or she does become your own," Colton answered. "My parents would be very offended if you claimed the contrary."

"What do you mean?" she asked, looking at him again.

"That we're more similar than you think, Grace."

He picked her up and brought her onto his lap to tell her what everyone in Elm Ridge knew but her.

"Landon and Julia adopted me when I was less than a year old," he explained. "My biological mother was my mom's kid sister Megan, and the father. Well, it seems no one's really sure who he was."

"Oh!" So much surprise was wrapped in a syllable.

Her eyes widened as she appeared to realize that he had

meant it. Adoption was really a viable option for him. He was not just saying it in an attempt to pacify or seduce her.

"Your mother—"

"—died at the tender age of seventeen."

"I'm so sorry," she said, resting her palm tenderly against his face. "So, so sorry."

"Don't be. I was very lucky. I had wonderful parents, and I found out earlier today that Ashton and Addison wanted to take me in as well. He said Mom wouldn't hear of it. So, there's nothing to be sorry about. I was always wanted and loved. Many children raised by their biological parents are not so lucky."

"You're right."

"I know I am," Colton confirmed, sounding a bit smug even to his own ears.

He leaned over to kiss her, and this time she kissed him back without any reservation.

They kissed forever like silly teenagers, and when they finally came up for air, he had to ask, "So counselor, are you resting your case?"

"Yes, I am, sir," she answered in a very businesslike tone. "And I've never been happier to be proven wrong."

"Then it's settled," Colton said.

"What do you mean it's settled?"

She frowned, as she clearly didn't understand where he was going with that.

"We're not getting any younger, are we?"

She tilted her head in agreement.

"And adoption processes are long and tedious."

She shook her head again.

"And anyone talking about adopting children should probably lay all their cards on the table."

Still sitting on his lap, she pushed back a little to take a better look at him and frowned.

Swallowing hard, he rushed forward. "I don't just care about you. I love you."

The frown slipped and slowly a smile took its place.

"You don't have to say anything. I understand if you want more time—"

She silenced him with her finger. "I don't need more time."

The heart that had been slamming madly against his rib cage stopped and his breath caught in his throat.

"I know what I want," she said softly. "You."

One word and his heart took off like a thoroughbred in a Kentucky field. "In that case. Counselor Baker, will you marry me?"

"You know I will, but," she hesitated, "maybe we should wait and see if you—"

Pressing his lips to hers, he silenced her with a kiss. The best way to settle a debate with his pretty lawyer.

A lawyer that would soon become a Kentucky Green.

CHAPTER 35

EPILOGUE

"I want to see that ring," Seated within earshot of Jaxon, Sandy Ball spoke loud enough for everyone to hear.

"Where are your manners," Chandi Nayar scolded her.

"I guess they flew out the window as soon as someone said the word diamonds," Gloria teased.

While the ladies at his table bickered, Jaxon watched Colton and Grace approaching. The two stars of the party were holding hands and grinning at each other like a couple of sappy teenagers. They both looked so happy, Jaxon barely recognized his brother.

All through their youth, Colton had been the broodiest of the Green kids. Grace had changed that. Somehow, she'd managed to make him lighten up. Nothing seemed too difficult for him. With Grace by his side, Colton appeared to be ready to conquer the world.

Grace came to a stop at the table. Sandy reached for her left hand and Colton's hand slid from hers to wrap casually around her waist.

"Wow, that's ... that's ..." Sandy was left speechless. That was a first.

But then again, Jaxon understood her loss of words. Colton had gone all in. The engagement ring on Grace's hand was impressive even to his own eyes. Jaxon didn't know anything about stones, or jewelry for that matter, but he could appreciate craftsmanship, and Grace's ring was a work of art. The diamonds were small but incased in a beautiful lace like setting.

"Buccelati," Gloria whispered in awe.

Ignoring her two friends, Dr Nayar took Grace's other hand in hers and whispered, "May you have many beautiful lifetimes together."

"That's the best wish ever!" Grace leaned into her new fiancé.

Staring down at his future wife as though she were the only person at the party, Colton silently nodded his agreement.

Jaxon felt a pang of envy. Would he ever feel that way?

Grace tilted her head so it came to rest on Colton's shoulder. His brother sighed with contentment and pressed his lips to the top of his future bride's head.

Would Jaxon ever love someone so much that the idea of spending not one, but several lifetimes with her wouldn't scare the living daylights out of him? Would his brothers look at him and know he'd fallen completely and totally head over boots for the perfect woman ?

"Imagine." Grace smiled. "Several life times would be just about the time we need to accomplish all the things we'd like to do. Visit all the places we want to see together."

Colton tightened his hold on Grace. "I'm not sure even that would be long enough."

The twins, Elizabeth and Faith sighed in perfect unison. Every woman at the table smiled at the two as if they were coveting a double scoop ice cream sundae.

Was this what he wanted ? And if it was, how did one know he'd found *the* one? How would he figure it out? What if he'd met her, and like a dunce, hadn't recognized it and let her escape?

Jaxon made a mental note to ask his brother when he had realized Grace was the one. Had he known right away when they had both met her by the fire?

"We have to make the rounds, " Grace said softly.

Colton chuckled. "Uncle Ashton is parading us around like a Kentucky Derby winner. "

Walking away, Colton grabbed hold of Grace's hand again —*was the man ever going to let go of her*—and tipping his head, whispered something in Grace's ear.

The woman blushed like a silly teenager. She'd changed too. Love had turned the serious lawyer into a playful young woman.

Shaking his head, Jaxon decided to adopt Colton's new take on life—everything would work out for the best. If the perfect woman for him was out there somewhere, he'd be the first to know. Wouldn't he?

I hope you've enjoyed Grace and Colton's story.

The rest of the Green clan is waiting for you.

GET JAXON HERE

If you keep on turning the page you'll get a "peek a book."

CHAPTER EXCERPT

JAXON

Jaxon braced himself and managed not to crush his cell phone. The big man took a deep breath and as calmly as he could asked, "Will you be there at eight tomorrow, so we can work out the discrepancies?"

Rita didn't answer right away. He could hear her breathing. She was still on the line. Patiently, he waited, but the only sound that came sounded like... a snore? Had she fallen asleep on him?

"Rita?" he asked softly, drawing on the very small reserve of patience he had left for this woman.

Despite the glowing recommendation she had provided, she was proving to be a disappointing hire.

"Rita!" he repeated more forcefully.

"Yes, yes, I heard you the first time," Rita replied, slurring her words.

Was she not sleeping but drunk?

A drinking problem would explain a lot of the issues she'd been having while running the kitchen of his facility. If that was the case, she would have to go. He couldn't possibly have an inebriated person working around the young children attending his new summer camp program. He felt for her—alcoholism was a real disease. But he couldn't trust her around a bunch of children if he couldn't trust her to be sober.

But if he fired Rita, how was he going to manage the kitchen?

"And no, I won't come on Monday. Hell, I won't come on Tuesday either. You know what, if you're gonna go behind my back to check the books, then I quit!"

"You what?" Miraculously, he managed to keep his tone civil. He wanted to unleash his wrath but had a feeling it wouldn't be productive. This entire conversation felt unproductive, just like the last few he'd tried to have with Rita.

Doubting he would be able to hold back for long, he left his mother's kitchen, where his sister Sophia and her best friend Willow were pulling a gigantic cake out of the oven.

"I quit," Rita repeated, words still slurring. "I won't work with someone who doesn't trust me, and that's all there is to it!"

The kitchen door slammed shut behind him, and Jaxon stomped toward his brother, and growled into his cell phone, "So that's it? You're leaving me hanging?"

The line went dead. Just to make sure, Jaxon checked his cell phone screen. Yep, she had hung up on him. It took a moment to get a handle on his anger, and he had to breathe calmly.

"Something wrong?" Colton looked up at him.

"The cook just quit," Jaxon tucked the phone away in his back pocket. "I've got ten kids arriving on Monday and double that the following week, and no one to cook for them."

"Time to pull out the Betty Crocker cookbook," his brother teased.

Jaxon was not amused. "I'd better go find a quiet spot to make some phone calls."

"Good luck," Colton called after him.

He'd need more than luck. Dropping on a bench by the back porch, he took in the large holiday gathering of friends and family. What a mess. He sucked in a deep breath and considered his options. None of which looked very promising.

Across the way his buddy Gunner looked in his direction. Too bad the guy didn't know his way around the kitchen the way he did around a horse. Laughing, Gunner's sister Mackenzie came up beside him followed by her two kids. They looked so happy. No one would have known that only a short while ago the two siblings had grown so alienated the only way they could talk to each other was with a lawyer. Fortunately, that lawyer had turned out to be Grace. The woman knew what she was doing. Now Gunner and Mackenzie were once again thick as thieves just as they'd been growing up.

At least he wouldn't have to worry about broken branches in his family tree. The Green family was tight—sometimes too tight possibly. But even when he had gone through his rebellious phase, Jaxon had never lost sight of his core value and priority: family came first. It saddened him to know not every family was like that.

The delicious scent of chocolate escaping through the kitchen door as it swung open again for Sophia and Willow distracted him from his thoughts about Gunner and his sister. Jaxon watched as Willow brushed a sheaf of hair from her eyes and then smiled at them. Warm and welcoming, she had a beautiful smile. Heck, everything about her was beautiful. Her personality was even more endearing than her looks. Right, but she was his sister's bestie. That made her off-limits for more than one reason.

"Come on," Sophia said. "Dad says the steaks are almost done.

Jaxon stood. Nothing like the promise of a nice juicy steak

to get a man moving. Jaxon He figured he'd be up from his deathbed with the right cut of meat seared to a perfect medium-rare. Good thing for him, his family liked to serve up the best beef, raised right on Green land. They served it at least once a week between Memorial Day and Labor Day. Sunday parties were a sacred tradition in the Green family, and it would take everyone coming down with the worst case of flu for one to be canceled.

Following tradition, on Memorial Day Jaxon's uncle, Ashton, had hosted the first party of the season with the assistance of his wife and six daughters. It had been a blast. Two of Jaxon's cousins were great cooks. Bailey had gone pro and, at the tender age of twenty-two, she was already a *sous chef* at Top Skewers, the best restaurant for miles around. Her sister, Audrey, was a great cook as well.

Maybe, Jaxon realized, Audrey could help with his problem. "Do you know if Audrey has anything planned for the rest of the summer?" Jaxon asked his sister as the small group made its way to the front lawn to meet with other guests.

"I'm not sure," Sophia answered. "Why do you ask?"

"'Cause my cook just quit." He didn't add that he probably would have fired her if she hadn't.

"Rita? Oh no. What's wrong with her? Is she sick?" Willow asked, voice full of concern.

Her question brought a smile to Jaxon's lips. This was typical of his sister's best friend—she cared about everyone. Sophia always said that Willow was one of those people for whom there are no strangers, only friends she had yet to meet. That summed her up pretty well.

"I'm not certain what's wrong with her," Jaxon confessed. Of course, he had a good idea, but sharing that felt too much like gossiping. He needed to focus on his problem, not on why it had happened. "I just know I'm in dire need of a cook."

"Then I guess you're in luck," Sophia said, grabbing his arm with a huge smile.

"I am?" He blinked at her. What was his sister up to?

"Yes, indeed. Don't you know that there's this amazing young woman in town and…" Sophia's smile grew wider "…she's been looking for a job all week. Guess what? It turns out she's a licensed nutritionist. And you need a cook. That sounds like a perfect match to me."

At the end of his sister's sentence, Jaxon's smile vanished as quickly as it had grown. Sophia's suggestion was a good one, but it wouldn't work for him. "I think I'll have to figure something else out."

"Why?" Sophia asked. She was getting those frown lines around her eyes that always revealed she was displeased, no matter how placid her expression otherwise.

"You just said she's a nutritionist. She's overqualified for the job," Jaxon answered. "I love the idea of giving the kids a balanced diet but, you know, this is just a summer camp thing. It's a new program, and I'm not charging the families enough to pay to keep a nutritionist on staff. The amount I'm charging will barely cover the cost of the program as it is."

"If it's money you're worried about, I would do it for Rita's salary," Willow interrupted, her expression earnest.

Jaxon stopped dead in his tracks and looked at the woman who had been attached at the hip to his sister ever since their freshman year of college. "*You're* the nutritionist?"

"Of course she is," Sophia answered for her friend. "And like me, she's also a nurse. But while I went on to become a nurse practitioner, Willow decided to branch out into something fun but still health-related—nutrition."

"It must have slipped my mind." Jaxon should have remembered.

"So, what do you say?" Willow asked, her eyes darting between Sophia and him. Hope shone in her eyes.

She seemed to be hanging on what he said next, which left Jaxon feeling pressured. Lord knew he wanted to have her around, which was precisely why he should find a graceful way to decline. He opened his mouth to do just that, but he couldn't bring himself to crush the optimism in Willow's expression.

"Please say yes!" Sophia pleaded. "Then she'll be able to spend the rest of the summer with us in Elm Ridge."

"Okay, fine," Jaxon said, raising his hands in surrender and turning toward Willow. "You're hired!"

"Thank you! Thank you, Jaxon!" Willow jumped into his arms. They tightened around him, making it hard to breathe, but not because she was squeezing too tightly. She was squeezing just right, and his brain was in overload from the sensations flooding him. Somehow, he hugged her back clumsily.

There was something about his sister's best friend that had always called out to him. Since Sophia had invited her to spend the summer with them a few years back, Willow had become a family fixture. She had been adopted not only by his brothers and their parents, but also by their cousins. She might fit in even better than Jaxon himself had during his rebellious phase.

As the years passed, Sophia and Willow had shed their tomboy attitudes to become more feminine, and right that instant, holding her that close, Jaxon second-guessed his impulsive decision.

Now that he thought about it, he wasn't sure anymore. Maybe working closely with her was not such a great idea. Being around Willow all the time would seriously press his ability to keep thinking of her as the young tomboy he'd met years ago. She was anything but now, and he doubted his ability to remain immune, or at least maintain the charade of being aloof.

Though there could be another way to look at the situation, he thought. So maybe it *was* a good idea. It was one way to make sure she remained off-limits. She would be his employee, after all. And that meant that no matter how tempted, he'd have to remember she worked for him. That should keep his thoughts on the straight and narrow.

He hoped.

"And you know," Willow said, letting him go, "Since your parents have so graciously invited me to stay for the summer, I'll be living rent-free. I could share my salary with Audrey if she needs the work as well."

Typical Willow again. Even though, as far as he knew, her financial situation was somewhere between precarious and desperate, she was willing to forego some of her newly-found income to share it with Audrey. Generous to a fault.

So pretty and so sweet. He wanted to hug her again. Not a good idea. So instead, he just nodded. "That's nice of you to offer, Willow. I'll see what I can do so no one has to share though." He'd already tweaked and stretched the budget to the snapping point, but it didn't sit right to have two women doing the work for the wage that would be fair for just one. And Audrey had been the first person to pop into his mind to ask for help.

She blushed and smiled before looking away in embarrassment. "Of course. I mean, it's no big deal."

The blush gave her such a pretty glow that the urge to hug hit him even harder. He swallowed hard and walked away toward the grill, mumbling about helping his other brothers out. In reality, he was the one who needed a helping hand—and maybe a lick of common sense. His brain told him having

Willow around was going to mean trouble, but his heart was set on ignoring that wise counsel. His body fell somewhere in between the two, but the traitorous thing was clearly leaning toward siding with his heart.

He had a feeling he was about to make a big mistake.

That didn't mean he was going to stop himself from making it.

GET JAXON HERE

Also should you want a copy of Gloria's cheat sheet, you know, the family tree she offered to Grace, just go to :

www.oliviasands.com/GloriasCS

and I will be happy to send it to you.

ABOUT THE AUTHOR

Olivia Sands is the happy mother of a certified geek and an adventurous veterinarian.

She writes contemporary sweet romance set in Elm Ridge, a fictitious small Kentucky town.

You can become a member of Olivia's **VIP readers group** to get goodies and news at https://oliviasands.com/BM

You can also follow Olivia on

* her site

https://oliviasands.com

* Facebook

https://www.facebook.com/OliviaSandsAuthor

* Instagram

https://www.instagram.com/oliviasandsauthor/

* Twitter

https://twitter.com/byOliviaSands

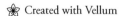

Made in the USA
Middletown, DE
19 July 2022

69697181R00119